No Hope

No Hope

TYRESS CUNNINGHAM

AHTRAE PUBLISHING, LLC

www.therealearthagatlin.com

Also by Tyress Cunningham

Conflict of Intere$t

To Kim Doss, my God Mother. I'm glad you got to see me turn my life around for the good.

And to my cousin Keisha, rest in peace~

No Hope

The child of envy bares a crooked smile.

~Street Scriptures

The name of the game changed. It went from getting money to murder. It's not about counting money, it's how many bodies you got, leaving us with no *hope*.

Chapter One

The day was gone, nobody was in the giving spirit and there was absolutely no cheer. This year on Christmas, crisp in white, old man winter showed up bitter and cold, tooting his own horn. Detestable temperatures chilled at a frigid eight degrees below zero. Sharp winds blew by, cutting the naked skin at ease with freeze, under the full moon and consumed in the city's light. The night was right despite the detrimental heat coming from the crime strangling the streets. Out and about, police were running circles around blocks trying to put a choke hold on the less fortunate out gambling with the odds of fate.

At the age of seventeen, he was young and standing in the snow. For him, anything was a go for the dough. His name was Hope and like so many others before him, he was taking a penitentiary chance trying to get it right. Wheat grain-colored boots covered his feet, insulated black leather gloves showed love for his hands. He wore a thick black goose feathered coat that kind of did the trick for concealing heat. What resembled smoke in the air was simply Hope's warm breath leaving his nostrils in the cold night. He was a dark soul without a heart. He had money on his mind and only a few bucks in his pocket along with some large knots of cocaine.

Hope's eyes spotted a few dollars, or what could be clear and potential danger, approaching him. In the game, money and danger were almost one in the same. You couldn't have one without the other. Never lacking and as a normal reaction, Hope clenched his heat which just so happened to be a FN-Five-SeveN holding numerous rounds in the magazine for ammunition just in case somebody was wishing for a good time. He stood firm concealing the weapon under the coat when the junkie with a monkey on his back and a jones in his bones, walked up on Hope and stood in front of him.

"What's the word, shorty? You workin'?" the junkie said while sliding up on Hope. Hope was young but that didn't mean he was dumb. His eyes glanced over the man standing in front of him, who damn near looked like an ice sculpture. Hope saw yellow *snot-cicles* hanging from the man's nose while also observing how poorly the junkie's coat was performing against the harsh winter elements.

Hope could clearly see where large holes had developed in the coat, exposing the junkie's dirty undergarments. At the same time, the junkie was taking in his own evaluation on the situation Hope was currently in. He'd never seen Hope on this particular block.

He knew this kid was way out of bounds and definitely out of his jurisdiction.

"Hmmm, aye shorty, I ain't never seen you post it up around here before. You new out here, huh? You sure you know what you doin'?" the junkie asked Hope with all sincerity. Then he continued to speak to Hope with caution.

"Dig this, shorty. Maybe you should yield a lil' bit, slow down and think about what you doin' because this shit out here is real, lil' nigga. It ain't no turning back, Jack. Just look at what it did to me!" the junkie testified voluntarily, as he gave the teenager a serious stare down as a warning. His yellow eyes told no lie of what the streets could do to you. The truth is this, life often offers you signs. It's on you whether you take heed or not, but keep in mind once you're told, it's on you if you remain blind.

Hope laughed, "Man, what the fuck is you talking 'bout? Huh, you trying to teach me a lesson? Is you a muthafuckin' teacher or something? Nah, nah, you must be a muthafuckin' preacher. Man, fuck that shit, it's too hot out here, police everywhere, for the god's honest truth. Is you shopping or what muthafucka'?" Hope laughed again, and got serious, getting ready to pop the shit outta him if the junkie wasn't going to shop.

"A'ight, shorty," the junkie said. Hope thought again about what the junkie said and once more laughed off the warning with arrogance. The voice of reasoning couldn't be heard. The only thing Hope could hear was that emptiness coming from his hollow pockets.

The junkie was slapped across the face with disrespect by the arrogant laughter coming from Hope. The junkie's face no longer showed signs of concern, nor did he care about safety measures in dealing with the teenager. The game was on. Hope just made it quite clear that he was down with the shit and he was definitely all in. The act of being belittled, when showing concern for the teenager, burned the junkie. He was hot and his conniving ways were underway. He wiped frozen snot-icicles from his tender nose and chose his words carefully. The junkie smiled.

"Shop, yeah I'ma shop. That's what I'm here for, what the fuck you think I'm standing in the cold fo'? That's what I do, shorty, ya hear me? I shop," the junkie said, reaching his nearly frostbitten hand into his pocket and pulling out plenty of crispy twenty-dollar bills to show Hope shit was real. Hope was quickly being hypnotized. The fresh green cash flashed across his eyes catching him by surprise. The junkie immediately recognized the glare in Hope's stare. He waved the money around with his right hand.

"Yeah, shorty, I spend money. This what I do. I smoke mansion and Lamborghini money baby. I spend all kind of money, and if ya' shits good, hey, I'll be back Jack," he explained making Hope feel alright about indulging in the economical negotiation for illegal commodities. Life lessons were always being taught, even when people weren't paying attention. Even when the outcome meant paying with their own life. See underestimating somebody could leave you a dead body, and nobody would even know it.

"A'ight, okay, cool what you trying to get?" Hope asked, relaxing his finger on the gun's trigger.

"Um, let me get…" while the junkie thought about his order, Hope's firm grip on the gun handle lightened in anticipation of the upcoming sale. This transaction about to take place would let him go in the house for a minute to warm up. Distracted by money and the urgent desire for warmth, Hope couldn't see it coming but he sure could feel it. He'd been warned already but because of principles Hope didn't yet fully understand, he found himself on the short end of the stick. The junkie dropped the money on the ground and went down to pick it up. He rose back up with a surprise.

He told Hope, "Everything lil' muthafucka'," while he held a razor-sharp, stainless-steel, hunting knife up to Hope's throat, initiating an armed robbery. Hope's helpless eyes watched the bait money suddenly vanish.

"See lil' nigga, I wasn't gonna rob you, but it's ya mouth," the junkie explained his motive. He slowly began to push the sharp blade into Hope's skin drawing blood for full corroboration.

"Take your muthafuckin' hands out your pockets," he quickly ordered Hope. Hope wanted to go for his gun but that wasn't an option. He could see in the junkie's eyes and hear it in his voice, that would get him killed quickly.

"Nigga, don't make me say it again," the junkie said, applying a little bit more pressure on the knife and the situation, drawing more blood.

"Ahhh!" Hope groped in pain and then began to do as he was told. He took his hands out his pockets and raised them in surrender. Amused and smiling now, the junkie was pleased with seeing fear in the arrogant teenager's face. Hope knew it was over, he didn't want no smoke.

"Ahhh, c'mon man. Just take the shit!" Hope made a free handed, free for all, plea bargain in exchange for his life. Hope could have cared less about the money and shit. He was trying to keep from getting knocked off. At Hope's request, the junkie was more than happy to oblige him.

"That's what you want me to do, huh?" the junkie said, shrugging his shoulders. Then he continued to adlib, "If that's what you want, a'ight then, that's what I'ma do." He began to aggressively yank items out of Hope's pockets. Still being pleasured with seeing fear in Hope's face, the junkie had questions for him.

"Take the shit, take the shit! Huh? Lil' nigga why I don't hear you laughin' now? Shit ain't funny, huh?" Hope's stomach was balling up while watching the junkie remove the few bucks and large knots of cocaine from his pockets. Then the junkie made a remarkable discovery.

"Oh! What is this?" the junkie wanted to know as he smiled, disarming Hope. He carefully took the FN-Five-SeveN off the teenager's hip. Being more of a knife man, the junkie put the gun comfortably on his own hip so he could sell it later and kept the knife right where it was, on Hope's throat. He kept talking to the teenager as he checked Hope's pockets.

"Do I look like a muthafuckin' teacher, little bitch? Do I look like I go to church? Give me this muthafuckin' shit!" the junkie said, demanding the money and respect. He had taken almost everything from Hope.

The sharp edge of the knife pressed into Hope's throat was hurting him badly, but it didn't hurt as much as his pride did. A tear was shed and nearly froze on his cheek, as it rolled down his face. Hope thought, *how the fuck am I about to lose my life with a knife for being so careless?* He couldn't believe he'd let this happen to him. He could feel the ice-cold hand of the junkie violating his pockets. The hand holding the knife didn't move. Hope could also feel blood running down his neck. The blade rested on Hope's vocal cords. Hope was about to become a mute. The junkie didn't want the teenager going back making a sound about who robbed him, so cutting the vocal cords in Hope's vocal box was law, but mercy was about to be shown.

"You know what? You are a lucky muthafucka'. I ain't gonna kill your lil' ass tonight, only because it's Christmas. I'm gonna let you live. But I better not catch yo' ass on this block no more. Nod your head if you understand what the fuck I just said, shorty." Hope did exactly what he was told. The junkie was telling him what it was and what it wasn't going to be. When Hope finished nodding his head, the junkie wanted to further humiliate the teen-ager and end the robbery with an exclamation point. He muffed Hope in the face, lifting him off his feet into the air and made him fall hard on the ashy-icy concrete.

"Muthafucka'," the junkie mumbled as he walked and stood over Hope. He looked at him with triumph. "Don't forget what I told you, lil' nigga, and for disrespecting me," the junkie coughed up green and yellowish mucus, then snorted it. As a reminder for the teenager's disrespect, he let a huge wad of snot and saliva fly out of his disgusting mouth. The huge glob of spit landed right in the middle of Hope's forehead.

Laughing, the junkie boasted, "Laugh at that wit' yo' bitch ass," and strutted off, feeling good. He felt so good he decided to sing "For the Love of Money," an old school, familiar tune by the O'Jays. While he was thinking about how he was going to enjoy the spoils of war, his night was about to be spoiled.

CLICK!

The junkie's singing and laughing came to an abrupt halt and he froze in his tracks at the sound of another gun being cocked behind his back.

The junkie wondered, *How da fuck I miss that?* Moving too fast and doing too much was about to leave him out of touch with reality. The *real* lesson on the streets was about to be taught. The junkie automatically knew when he heard another gun getting ready to explode and shoot him that his small victory would be short lived. There was no mercy in the streets. A small revolver at hand and role reversal had Hope up and the junkie down on his luck.

"Nah, man, ain't gonna be a next time," Hope said before the first gunshot rang out. *BAH!* The hot lead hit the junkie in the buttocks, knocking a patch out his rotten ass.

"Aaahh!" he screamed out loud from the hot shot and spun around. "Wait…"

BAH!

Hope shot again, knocking the air out of him. His aim game was on point. He hit him directly in the chest. The junkie dropped to the ground, falling over in the snow, grabbing his chest trying to catch his breath. Hope's finger paused on the trigger; his heart was thumping in his throat. His young eyes watched the man who'd robbed him and threatened his life lay in the snow trying to fight. He saw dark blood spurt through the junkie's fingers flamboyantly staining the pure white snow.

There was no time to waste, he ran up and looked down on the dying man struggling with the reality that he was about to be moving on up the rough side of the mountain. The junkie was making gurgling sounds trying to talk. He was choking on his own blood and groaning, not wanting to let go of life. He was trying to pray but couldn't. Every time he tried to speak, blood filled his mouth and he couldn't breathe. Hope showed no sympathy whatsoever in his eyes. He leaned over and rammed the cold steel barrel of the gun into the junkie's mouth, shattering teeth, and pulled.

BAH! The gun exploded.

"Fuck wrong with you," Hope said.

That was it, that was all, the monkey was off the junkie's back, and the jones was gone in his bones. For letting such filthy things fly out his mouth he had to bite the bullet. Hope blew the junkie's entire mouth off. He wiped the spit off his face and bent down to start on his recovery. He took back every-single-thing that belonged to him from the dead man's body.

He also snatched the junkie's money, too. In the process of his search, Hope could hear police sirens. He tucked both guns and began to run. The footprints he left behind in the snow were running from jail and death. He left *no hope* for the man lying in the bloody snow to survive, and with this second body under his belt, there definitely was *no hope* for his future, but one thing was certain: he was going to keep *Hope* alive.

One-Illinois.
Two-Illinois.
Three-Illinois.
Four-Illinois.
Five-Illinois.
Six-Illinois.
Seven-Illinois.

Eight-Illinois seconds passed before the Rockford police task force showed up on the new murder scene to stand around with their arms crossed, shooting the breeze and trying to suppress their laughs in front of the local news cameras. In silence, the red and blue lights on top of police vehicles flashed in the coldness of night. Nosey people who would never talk to the police came out of their homes slipping and sliding across the sleek ice on the street, almost busting their ass moving fast trying to see the after-effects of the gunshots ringing outside their windows. Only to have their curiosity curbed by yellow caution tape set up from light pole to light pole at the latest homicide in what's called the most dangerous small city in America when they made it to the scene. The temperature may have been low, but the murder rate was at an all-time high. Dark blood drastically decorated the white sheets laying over the deceased for censorship, matching the bloody snow.

"So, who hit the eternal lottery tonight, guys?" the head detective nonchalantly asked the surrounding officers as his boots made a crunching sound in the snow. He began to cool off his coffee by blowing the steam coming from the dark cup of Joe he was holding in one hand before taking a sip. He squatted down to lift the bloody sheet with the other hand, so he could get a good peak at the victim.

"Oh wow, you…somebody finally *gotcha ass,* huh? Damn and they gotcha good, too," the head detective said, talking slick to the deceased before he could even begin to rest in peace. As though the dead man could really hear his sarcasm. This wasn't the first time he'd seen a man lying dead in the snow. In his rookie years, and throughout his career, the head detective had many run ends with deceased junkies.

This homicide victim was a well-known parasite throughout the murky neighborhood. The head detective wasn't surprised to see him lying there, but what did surprise him was the fact that the frozen rat hadn't been whacked years back. Slim Pickins was the deceased victim's government name, but he was known on the streets as Slim. He acquired the name because he had a bad habit of taking a pinch off other people's hard-earned profits. His criminal activities neither here or there, always had Slim either an arrest from the cage or an inch from the grave. The head detective held the cup of coffee but pointed his middle finger to count the gunshot wounds.

"Let me see here, uh, one, two, and three. Who did you piss off to have a gun shot inside your mouth, huh?" the lead detective said, letting the bloody sheet fall back over the junkie's damaged face. He stood back up and took a sip of coffee, then he looked around to survey the area. This crime scene was no different than any other one he'd seen before. If he'd seen one dead nigga, he'd seen them all. He looked back down to consider all the factors that played a part in the deceased's untimely departure.

"Hmm, no shell casings anywhere, and your pockets turned out like an eighteen-year-old prostitute shooting up heroin." He was trying to find some type of evidence that would corroborate with the crime scene. "So that means you robbed the wrong person this time, you piece of shit, and they must have come back for their shit and you tried to play tough," he spoke. Then the lead detective began to quickly come up with a thesis for the matter laying in front of him.

"You should have slowed down a long time ago, now just look at you." The lead detective continued to talk to the dead man, even though he knew his words were falling on deaf ears. Then he considered the deceased man's character. "Yeah, I know you, that's what you did. You played tough, didn't you? Now, I gotta solve your murder. Hmmm, good luck. We'll both see how that turns out, but I'ma tell you now, don't hold your breath on that one," the lead detective laughed, already bringing closure to the cold case. "Hey, one of you guys call the coroner. Something's starting to stink about this case," he ordered the other officers standing around the crowded crime scene left behind by Hope.

Chapter Two

"Take as much time as you need, I know this is very difficult for you, ma'am." Gospel music softly played in the background on a loudspeaker for comfort, but the funeral director thought *where's the comfort in burying your child?*

"Ma'am, ma'am," he spoke to the grief-stricken woman with gentleness in his tone. The tall slim well-dressed funeral directors dark suit matched the mood in the dim, candle-lit room. Smooth, freshly polished caskets of all colors were out on display, sitting in front of the sobbing young mother waiting to be put on an installment plan. "Ma'am I'm going to take your son's suit to the back, to give you a little more time, okay?" he said, picking up the suit laying over a chair next to her.

"Oh, God! He's gone, my baby's gone!" she screamed when she saw him walk away with her son's burial suit. The horrible screaming coming from the grieving young mother brought tears to her family members who were trying to be strong and support her. Sadness and broken hearts could be seen in all their facial expressions.

"Why! My nephew, Lord, why him, Lord?" her sister cried out.

The funeral director eased back on the scene and offered the older lady a box of Kleenex as her cries haunted the funeral home.

"Here ma'am, please take this."

He moved and spoke with complete professionalism even though it was hard for him to erase the thought of the young boy's death. As he entered the room, he was met by a storm of tears drowning the room. The realization hit him, it was the day after Christmas, her son had been smoked a week and a half ago. The grieving mother stopped crying for a second and sat weeping as she was surrounded by other grieving loved ones, they all looked lost due to her tragic loss. She was trying to find her way to make the funeral arrangements for her baby. The game had taken her sons innocence, but Hope had taken her son's life. Her son was in the streets playing the role and that's how the police found him. He had been gunned down and found crawled up under a car in the snow.

The story was all over the news and talked about in all four public high schools. Kids in schools were reading books, talking about death, learning the real meaning of subtraction, and history in the streets. The lady's son was the hottest topic in the city. That was until last night, before a junkie had been found slain in cold blood. It was the second murder in less than two weeks.

Meanwhile, she wept in front of the funeral home. Unfortunately, her son had been the first-person Hope killed. The nine-year-old boy was supposed to be in school, but he laid on a steel examination table, in the back of a funeral home with his eye lids permanently superglued together forever. He was stretched out cold and naked with large Y-stitchery sewn across his skinny torso. Only a shell of a nine-year-old African American boy remained to be injected with embalming fluid, for viewing purposes.

The very skilled middle-aged mortician was trying her best to repair the fatal body damage. She was making Hope's first homicide victim look as if he died in asleep. Although this was her profession, it was hard to perform her professional duty because the client lying before her was the very same age as her own son. At the mere thought, her eyes teared up.

"Oh Lord, help me get through this. You are my strength," she prayed with watery eyes and a torn heart, as she worked magic on the young man's body. The mortician lady was making preparation for her client to look like he was resting in peace for a homegoing ceremony while thinking about her own son, who she hoped sat in biology class listening to a science teacher who stood at a chalkboard. She visualized her son, concentrating, and taking notes, preparing to pass an upcoming biology test, so she would grant him permission to go to the high school homecoming dance. Life was about choices and chances, and she continued to hold back her tears. She made the choice to do her job to the best of her abilities, so the family would have a chance to see the boy at rest.

While in front of the room, the funeral director stood by a beautiful black casket with an all-black silk interior and a pillow covered in white silk. He allowed them to take as much time as they needed. Suddenly, his display of patience and compassion for the mourning young mother who was about to cash out on her baby was interrupted by someone he knew as she walked into the establishment. The elderly lady strolled in slowly holding onto a wooden cane. Her wrinkle face showed sorrow, but her stature showed grace. He quickly moved in the woman's direction. The mourning young mother and family didn't pay him any attention because of their grief.

As he headed toward the elderly woman and before he could greet her with the proper respect, she spoke, "Well God done called him home last night. Seeing his days are determined, the number of his months are with you; you have appointed his limits, so that he cannot pass. Look away from him that he…"

"May rest," the funeral director finished reciting the scripture from Job chapter fourteen verses five and six. She gave him a warm southern smile. Her gold teeth shone behind her hurt.

"The way he lived I was blessed to have him for so long," she spoke with a slight southern accent.

"Slim was…" he stopped short of what he was about to say. "I'm so sorry. I mean your son was a good person at heart but those drugs, those drugs. Those drugs are what.. well, I'll say it this way, your prayers every night are what kept your son alive for so long—"

She cut him off, "I know, but you always stayed his friend."

Then the small talk was over. She wasn't there for personal reasons. She was there on business. The elderly lady reached in her purse and pulled out a stack of cash. She'd prepared herself for this moment. That's why the crying from the other family in the room didn't bother her. She had cried for her own son long ago.

"Huh, take this baby. I see you're busy now. I'll be back," she said, giving him a hug. There was nothing he could say. He had been friends with her son since childhood.

"Yes ma'am, I'll be here, and I'll start making arrangements as soon as I'm done with this family," he assured her. She walked out the door and the young mother and her family's cries continued to fill the room.

"Why! Why, God!"

Chapter Three

A week had passed and surrounding the glass table diamonds were being cut.

"Play another one with ya' card playing ass," Cap said while smoothly letting the nine of spades slide across the glass surface of the table. The audience watched the intense card game and snickered at the slick talk. Hope's eyes cut across the room to see who was laughing at his expense. Sitting at the card table and losing his money, shit didn't seem too funny to him. It's always outside influences that normally get shit kicked off, but that wasn't the case.

"Uh, muthafucka'!" Cap yelled with the utmost confidence as he stood up from his seat and slapped the Ace of Spades across the glass table, making the playing card fly off the table and straight into Hope's chest. At Hope's expense, the onlookers once again broke out into laughter. He took the card that seemed to grow wings and landed it back on the table, where it belonged.

"Aye, nigga, keep that muthafuckin' card on the table," Hope spoke words of wisdom to Cap, and stopped everyone from laughing at the same time.

"Damn baby, what he think he doing? Checking somebody or something? Uh, where they do that at?" Cap's beautiful, rich, chocolate skin toned girlfriend voiced her opinion.

Cap looked back at his beautiful queen and then shot an evil eye in Hope's direction. Then he began to comfort his woman, "Nah, baby he wouldn't be sitting in here doin' no sucha thing," Cap said, pulling out his black Glock .40 laying it on the glass table with the barrel facing Hope's direction for reassurance. She smiled at Hope, while standing behind her man's chair.

Hope's card playing partner sat back from the table. "Holdup, Cap. Man whatcha' on? A muthafucka ain't here for that. A nigga just tryin' to win some money and go home fam'. You ain't gotta be uppin' your pistol and shit." Cap took his evil stare off Hope and laid it on him, since he wanted to get in the business.

"Nigga, who told you to say something, huh?" Cap sat his playing cards on the table and picked up the Glock .40 as he stood.

"Huh? Who da fuck said you could say something?"

The audience was standing on thin ice watching the new development at the card game. Orange flames from several blunts being inhaled flashed across the room. The strong marijuana smoke was floating across Cap's face as he stood under the light hanging over the glass card table. Hope's card partner was sitting there looking dumbfounded and nervous.

"What's wrong now? You can't talk? You was just talkin' like a muthafucka, now you can't talk all of a sudden," Cap kept drilling him and waving his gun around.

"Nah, Cap, man I was just sayin'," Cap stopped him mid-sentence when he put the Glock .40 directly in his face.

"You was sayin' what?" Cap yelled at the card player. The thunder in his voice made everyone in the room jump.

"Wait! Wait! C'mon. Cap don't shoot me man. I'm sorry man, I'm sorry."

Hope sat there looking from across the table with disgust. He couldn't believe this nigga was performing like this. Cap had everyone in the room shook up something decent and on top of that, he was real dedicated to his performance. Instead of Hope being somewhere ducked off laying low and letting the heat on the street cool off, he found himself in another fucked up situation where he was going to have to sleep yet another nigga. All because a nigga wanted to show off in front of his instigating nothing ass bitch, and everybody else in the room. Hope acted like nothing was happening and played his card. A two of spades left from his fingertips and slid across the glass table stopping next to the ace of spades. Although Cap had Hope's card playing partner held at gunpoint, making his point come across blatantly, Cap changed his focus when he saw the two of spades out of the corner of his eye slide next to his card on the table. This seemed to humor him because he laughed.

"Now see, that's what I'm talkin' 'bout," Cap said, lowering his gun out of Hope's card partners face. "Let's get back to the card game. I ain't finished taking your money. But aye, you nigga," Caps said specifically pointing the black Glock .40 at Hope's card playing partner again, "Get out your body one more time in this muthafucka' and I'ma leave ya ass like they found that dope fiend ass nigga Pitch the other night. I'ma blow your fucking mouth off, ya hear me?" Cap told him, then sat back down and placed the gun back on the table.

"It's on you. Play a card, any card. This our book. They ain't got shit, they can't beat this," Cap said to his own card playing partner who was still sitting on stuck, and the look on his partners face seemed to piss him off a little bit.

"What the fuck you lookin' scared fo', play a goddamn card. You actin' like I was gonna pop yo' ass. Nigga, you wit' me?" Cap reminded his partner and everybody in the room went back to laughing.

Everyone was laughing it up. Yep everybody except Hope. Hope and a skinny, flashy dressing crook standing in the room looking to capitalize on the moment in order to seize a little pleasure with a few choice words.

"Hey baby, these niggas is tweaking in this bitch," he said looking over the shoulder of the female standing in front of him.

The bait had been laid. If she looked back, that meant she wanted to play. Her head turned to see who was talking behind her.

"You looking back to see who's gonna save you?" he asked her under all the noise in the room. He saw her eyes light up when she noticed the gold jewelry hanging from his neck and accompanying his wrist and fingers. He knew she was sold on the idea of being saved.

"Aye, let me talk with you, while I walk with you." The recently released convict named Wiggles advanced his hand, giving her a chance to save herself from all this madness in the room. She didn't say not one word, nor did she hesitate to take his hand and follow his lead. They walked through the crowd smoking weed, drinking, and watching the card game. Wiggles could feel a few people laying eyes on his prize catch, as they moved accordingly. She walked behind him not minding all the attention. She wasn't concerned about that. She was undressing Wiggles with her mental state.

"Yeah, in here, come on," Wiggles said, as he walked her into the bathroom, cut on the lights and closed the door behind them. He stood there admiring all the natural gifts she had been blessed with. She had bedroom eyes, a cinnamon brown skin tone, her lips looked sweet, and her thighs were thick and inviting as she held her hand on her hip. It was time for him to give the proper introduction.

"What's your—" she put her index finger up to his lips cutting his words off by the roots.

"Shh, no names, let me see you pull it out." When she told him that, he knew right then it couldn't get no better than this. Wiggles could see by the look in her eyes and the way she was standing there in great anticipation waiting and wanting to see his dummy that she was a freak, and she was ready to get real wild and rambunctious on the dick. But he knew she didn't know exactly who she was fucking with. Wiggles was the truth, and she was about to find out how honest he truly was.

"Okay how about this? Since we don't know each other, how about we peel and reveal at the same time?" She shook her head in disagreement.

"Uh-huh, pull it out," she said, making him play her game.

He wasn't about to go back and forth with her.

"Okay, cool," he said, unbuckling his five-hundred-dollar designer belt. He watched her eyes stay below his belt. He reached in his pants.

"Walla," he said, pulling out his business for her to see. She was taken aback when her eyes saw what he was really worth.

"Damn boy. I don't know about this, you is, mmhmm…" she was at a loss for words, "that's too big for me," she declared.

Wiggles looked at her and laughed, he was a 'P', he was a player not a phony. He began to place his joint back in his britches. The freak in her wasn't about to let her pass up this moment.

"Okay, hold on. I'ma do this, but you gotta promise me you ain't gonna hurt me, a'ight?" she said, giving him a worried look. "Okay?" she asked him. Then she went and unbuttoned her skin-tight blue jeans. She was watching him pull his shit back out and get ready to do damage. "You promise?" she asked again nervously. While she was unzipping her tight jeans hugging her hips making sure he was going to stick to the agreement, he already knew what his reply was going to be.

"Uh, yeah sure. I promise," he tried to win her trust with a dishonest smile. Evidently, she was convinced because his eyes marveled at how beautiful and soft her thighs looked as she slowly struggled pulling her pants down. That's when he discovered that there were no panties involved in this removal procedure. Then all of a sudden, they both heard a knock on the door and saw the tarnish doorknob turning rapidly.

"Aye! Aye! Muthafucka', somebody in here. Y'all gotta go outside!" Wiggles yelled and then grabbed the half-dressed thick girl by her waist and guided her to the front of the sink in the bathroom.

Although the knocking on the door didn't stop, neither did Wiggles and what was about to go down. He bent her over the sink with the dripping faucet. She looked back at him while leaning over the sink.

"Remember you promised me?" she reminded him looking into his eyes.

"What you mean? Be cool I got this; I know what I'm doin'," he told her. She turned her head, bracing herself. He took the initiative to slowly slide up inside her. He felt her tight wet walls open up for business on his behalf. She moaned knowing there was more to come.

"Ooooh baby." When Wiggles heard her soft cry of pleasure, he went inside her a few more inches deep. She started breathing a little bit harder. But she knew there was more to come and at that very thought she became wetter and wetter.

"Ahh, ahh," she moaned more, and he started stroking her rhythmically. He could see her making fuck faces in the mirror hanging on the wall over the sink. "Ahh-ahhh-shit," she was taking it from behind letting him get the pussy how he wanted. With every stroke now she could feel his dick going in deeper and deeper. She was being pressed hard between the sink and him and she was loving every minute of it. Wiggles was about to start standing up in the pussy. He felt her getting hot and bothered so he went to pounding it out and she wasn't ready for that because in the mirror he saw her eyes widen in pain. She tried to jump up, but his hands wrapped around her waist. He kept her in place and he began to go to work.

"Unh, unh, unh, unh, wha'tha fuck!" she moaned and asked questions but it was too late. There was no getting away from it, so she held onto the sink with both hands as he held onto her waist. He wasn't playing around at all, he was fresh out of prison, and she was going to feel it. Her moans became louder, and he was pounding her harder.

"Ahh-ahh baby you promised," she cried out as he kept on pounding, and he could feel her getting real messy. "You promised baby," she moaned gripping the sink with all her strength. He grabbed her by her hair.

"Bitch shut up," he told her and started going in deeper and harder. Wiggles was blowing her back out. She started shaking, her legs were giving out on her. The sink was the only thing holding her up.

"Aah-aah-aah-ooh God!" she screamed. She couldn't control her body any longer. Wiggles kept pounding her and he could feel her letting herself go as her warm body fluids started dripping down her weak and shaking legs.

"Awe fuck!" he groaned as he pulled his dick out her wet dripping pussy and shot thick white cum all over her ass. He lifted her up as she was still holding onto the sink breathing hard.

"You good?" he asked as if he gave a fuck. She couldn't say a word because she was still in mode.

He walked over, grabbed a towel off the shelf, wiped off his dick and threw it on the floor, then got himself together and walked out the bathroom. He slid past a line of people waiting outside the bathroom door that had been listening to them.

Wiggles didn't even bother closing the door behind him. The people waiting in the line saw the damage that had been caused. As they stood there looking at the girl with her pants still pulled down hanging onto the sink in shambles with his DNA running down her thick brown ass, Wiggles left her behind. He went back to watching the niggas gambling at the table playing Spades. He put himself in perfect position to catch one of the many blunts being passed around the room.

"Let me hit that," Wiggles said, making an interception. The weed was passed, and he put the strong smelling blunt up to his lips and inhaled deeply, letting the thick gray smoke entangle his lung tissue. "Wha'tha fuck?" Against his will the marijuana smoke forced Wiggles to cough. Although he was going through a violent tantrum, Wiggles wasn't going to let that stagnate his growth. He engaged himself once more.

Still coughing, he continued, "Huh, take this shit and kill ya'self," he said passing the blunt to the next victim in the room. Then he felt someone softly tugging on his shirt from behind. Wiggles turned around and from behind his heavy eyelids, he could see the girl from the bathroom looking at him smiling with lust in her eyes.

"Ke-Ke," she said to him. Wiggles looked at her like she was crazy.

"What?" he asked.

She said it again, "Ke-Ke, my name is Ke-Ke." Wiggles was about to say something but all the loud talking from the card table grabbed his attention. He turned his head back to see what was going on.

The game of Spades looked to be coming to an end. Cap had one more card left in his hand. "It's ah muthafuckin' wrap! Pay up niggas! Pay me my muthafuckin' money!" Cap yelled excited with his victory. He slapped the last card down on the table hard. Once again, the playing card flew off the glass table but this time it missed and flew past Hope.

Hope was pissed, he had lost seven bands, seven thousand dollars. That was a decent amount of money to just be losing. He couldn't trip though, losing was part of the game. It was just something he was going to have to honor. Hope sat there, low-key looking sick at the table. His stomach was hurting as he watched Cap endanger himself by boasting and flamboyantly raking up the mountain of money off the table.

"Card dummies, straight card dummies, baby. Them niggas is card dummies," Cap's girlfriend said out loud for everybody to hear as she helped her man collect his winnings. Right then, for some strange reason the room became silent to Hope. He could see people's mouths moving and smiling but he couldn't hear talking or laughter. He couldn't hear anything at all.

Then Cap changed all that by his next move. "Y'all know what? This little money ain't shit. Wha'tha fuck I'ma do with this little shit? Know what, huh!" Cap proclaimed, then he stood up and threw all the money he had just won into the thirsty crowd of people who were watching the card game. Seven thousand dollars went flying up into the ceiling in the cloudy room. Then the money broke up into change as it fell on the crowd of people like confetti. One, five, ten, and twenty-dollar bills were falling all over the place. It was straight havoc in the place. People in the room went into a frenzy as they reached out with open hands trying to snatch as much cash as possible. People were struggling and fighting with each other and those that fell to the floor in the mayhem were being trampled by the heavyweight of greed.

Hope could honor losing the card game, but he wasn't about to have his name attached to this. Just like the sucka Cap was playing him for, that's just what Hope needed. Through the thirsty crowd Hope could see Cap's Glock .40 still sitting on the table unaccounted for. With his gun on the table and his head turned admiring the chaos he had caused; Cap was now an open target. His pride had left him vulnerable for what was yet to come. Nobody was paying Hope any attention as he slowly removed his FN-Five-SeveN that held numerous rounds in the magazine for ammunition off his hip, for moments like this. People were running back and forth across the room until a gunshot rang out and stopped all movement.

"Blocka!" Everybody ducked to the floor with goosebumps still clenching their filthy palms with free money. All eyes were on Hope aiming his weapon at a still bullet hole free Cap. It was quiet as a courtroom, while court was about to be held in the streets. Cap stood only inches from his Glock .40, but it might as well have been ten miles away because nothing could help him now and he knew it, too. His helpless and watery eyes stared at the gun on the table then his eyes went up to look at Hope silently as he begged for mercy.

Hope observed the current situation and noticed that Cap's smart mouth girlfriend wasn't proudly standing next to her man anymore. Matter of fact, the truth be told, she was ready to switch sides. Now that Hope had Cap right where he needed him to be, he was about to make his opening statement.

"I wasn't gonna fuck you up, but yo' bitch ass been talking shit all night. You just couldn't shut the fuck up. Like a nigga told me before, it's ya mouth," Hope told him, while seeing the fear in Cap's facial expression. Not only that, but Hope could also see that Cap felt singled out and Hope didn't want him to feel that way because he wasn't alone.

"Yeah, nigga, ya' mouth. Yep, you and that raggedy ass bitch, standing behind you," Hope reminded them both, while walking over and picking up Cap's Glock .40 off the table. Then he pointed the black Glock .40 at Cap's girlfriend. She screamed so loud that she could have shattered the glass table if it wasn't so thick. Which made Hope laugh.

"Ha, ha, ha ha, get tha fuck out of here. Is you fa real? Ha, ha," he continued to laugh. Then Hope quickly gathered himself and got back on a serious note.

"Bitch you funny as fuck." Then with the gun still in Cap's face, Hope looked at Cap and specifically gave him orders.

"Nigga, you betta not move, boy." Hope walked past Cap and slapped the fuck out of his girlfriend with the Glock .40 across her face, making her fall straight to the floor screaming. Cap flinched and watched Hope standing over his lady. He could hear his girlfriend crying from the pain. Hope still had Cap at gunpoint, cross examining him.

"You wanna show out in front of this bitch, huh?" The look on Cap's face said it all. Then Hope cross examined Cap's girlfriend.

"What's tha matter, whatcha crying fo'? Tell ya nigga to help you," Hope said. Then he looked at everybody who was just laughing at him because of her smart-ass comments earlier. He watched all their faces change from humor to humility.

Hope was going to change their facial expression one more time, by giving them a real reason to watch their mouths. He lined his foot up correctly and kicked Cap's girlfriend smack dab in the center of her face as if he was a punter on a football team. Blood splattered all over his white shoes. Everybody in the room gasped at what they saw. Cap wanted to rush him but looking down the barrel of the FN-Five-SeveN made him stand still.

"Cap do something!" she screamed from down on the floor severely bleeding.

"Bitch what…" Hope mumbled underneath his breath in amazement. Then he drew his leg back, kicked her in the face again and kept on repeatedly kicking her in the face until blood was everywhere and she stopped screaming. Cap's girlfriend was knocked out cold from the trauma. Her head was moving from the contact, but she was definitely out cold. Her light switch was shut off. But to Hope that out cold shit could have just been an act. Just because she wasn't moving, didn't mean anything to him. Hope continued to swing his leg back and kick her in her shit. Out of the corner of his eye, Hope could see the people on the floor getting squeamish and queasy.

POW!

He shot off another round but this time it was from the Glock .40, which left Cap grabbing his shoulder. Hope had popped him. Cap fell on the floor next to his bloody unconscious girlfriend while trying to hold his shoulder in place.

"Ahhhh, ahhh!" Cap yelled in pain and fear. Hope stood over him.

"Shut yo bitch ass up," he said, as he lined his foot up in position with the bloody shoe and kicked Cap smack dab in the center of his face. Cap's nose exploded and blood shot everywhere. The impact made him release his hands from his shoulder and he laid stretched out. Hope drew back and kicked him again.

"Mutha fucka," Hope mumbled and then started stomping on the man's head. That's when he heard police sirens outside the house. He stopped badgering the co-defendants, then gave orders to everybody in the house, "Get the fuck outta here!" he yelled and went to shooting in the air.

BLOCKA! BLOCKA! POW! POW!

Both guns were going off, as people ran to the front door. He made his way out the back door to exit into the cold night. Everybody but Wiggles did as they were told.

He stayed back to collect as much cash as he could before the police entered the house. He made sure that he didn't step in any blood puddles. He moved around the bloody unconscious couple lying next to each other waiting for the police to discover them and call for medical assistance. Wiggles even went so far as to help Cap out. He went through his pockets and removed the rest of the money and found a bottle filled with some sort of pills.

"See, nigga I just help your goofy ass out," Wiggles said to him and continued to pick money up off the floor that wasn't tainted with their blood. Then he made his way out the crime scene through a side window of the house.

Chapter Four

"Lord knows this should have not happened! And epidemic is taking place right before you and me!" said the minister standing in the church while looking at the devastating faces in the sanctuary, the tall bulky and prestigious man's loud voice was reaching out to every ear in the overly crowded church. His long arms reached out over the large wooden podium engraved with a cross.

"Do you see this? This is what our children, our sons, have to look forward to, in the Black community. This right here! Right here! Here before us!" the minister prophesied and pointed his finger in the direction of an open polished black casket with gold trimming. On showcase, there was a boy lying there in an all-white suit with black pinstripes with his head resting forever on a silk white pillow.

Sorrow seized the moment and horrifying cries came from trembling lips that serenaded the church while heavy tears poured down saddened and painted faces like a rainstorm trying to drown out the pain in hopes to purify the wounded souls. A countless number of family and friends sat shoulder to shoulder on the torn fabric of the old squeaky wooden pews, as others stood tightly squeezed together feeling the pressure of their loss.

"Mothers in this city giving birth, having to turn right around and bury their baby in the dirt!" the minister spoke with grief looking down on the young weeping mother on the front pew as she barely held on to life as she knew it. Even if she wanted to hear the minister preach, she couldn't because the hurt in her heart wouldn't allow it and the minister knew it, but he continued his sermon.

"An epidemic! The young and old, no one's exempt. Black men are being murdered, young and old. Bullets are flying around with no age limit. Today, I'm standing here preaching at this young man's funeral and guess what? I'm not done because in a few more days I'll be standing in another church preaching at another funeral for a middle-aged Black man who was murdered on Christmas night! Do y'all hear me! A man murdered on Christmas night!" the minister yelled into the black microphone he was holding in one hand and in the other, he was holding back perspiration, as he wiped sweat off his forehead with a colorful handkerchief that matched his expensive suit and tie.

"An epidemic is lying before us!" he repeated, then paused for a second and took a deep sigh. The minister looked in the casket at the discolored boy and just dropped his head.

"Violence in our streets is shedding blood like a waterfall," he whispered softly into the mic with his head still held low. Then he took the handkerchief and dabbed at the corner of his eye, wiping away his own grief. He lifted his head, and tears could be seen as he tried to hold them back.

"If y'all don't mind, I would like to share with you what happened to me last night," the minister said to the congregation.

"Go ahead! Preach. Amen," the few amens and cheering coming from the family and friends in the church were an indication for him to carry on with the message he was trying to deliver. Then he began to fill the congregation in on how the current events from the past three weeks had impacted him to the point where he couldn't sleep at night. The minister took a deep breath and let go.

"Last night I was awakened from my sleep as the phone rang and rang. I picked it up and immediately heard crying and fear in this woman's voice. She was hysterical but she wanted to make reservations. Reservations for what, I wondered. Well, last night her son and her son's girlfriend were both beaten up badly and on top of being beaten, her son was shot. She was sitting in a hospital in the waiting room unsure if her son was going to make it or not and she wanted to make reservations just in case he didn't pull through. Right now, my heart is going out to you mothers. Now, to show how God works, this morning my phone rings and it's the same mother talking and sounding more calm, informing me that her son was going to live, but an epidemic is here and it lies right before us."

The minister spoke about another mother's good fortune and set off a reaction unlike no other.

"Ahh, ahh!" she yelled. The young mother dressed in an all-black dress and a veil covering her face tried to jump up from her seat. The family members were struggling to restrain her.

"My baby! They killed my baby! Oh God, why? Oh God why'd you do this to meee? No, no, my baby. You can wake up. Come on, wake up boy!" she continued to burst out screaming, interrupting the ministers prewritten, rehearsed sermon.

"Ah…let me go so I can get my baby!" she yelled at the top of her lungs as family and friends bore witness to the strength of the mother's love. The young mother broke free from the arms of those who undermined her love for her son, rushed the open casket and grabbed her deceased baby lying in it. She reached in.

"Come on! Wake up, let's just go home!" She was pleading with him as she held his cold discolored body next to her warm, soft, and loving skin. The whole scene shook the other mothers in attendance to the core of their soul. They quickly grabbed their own children and held them close to their hearts. The other mothers in the church were looking up to the heavens with tears in their eyes and were thanking God for His mercy upon them. They kissed their own children showing their appreciation and dreading ever having to go through this type of experience themselves. Little wide-eyed kids were shivering in their mother's arms as they covered their little ears trying to block out the screams coming from the lady upfront digging in the black casket

"Ah, come on baby wake up! God, please let my baby wake up!"

Although God could see and hear her cries there was absolutely no hope it was going to happen because it wasn't in His plans.

"Wake up!" she continued to yell in the casket tugging on her son. "Please baby wake up. Mommy's not mad at you just wake up!"

Chapter Five

There was a homegoing service taking place across town. It was two o'clock in the day, extremely cold, and busy in the waiting room of the hospital. Doctors hurried from room to room checking on their near dead patients. She was uncomfortable in a seat and her nerves were on edge. She didn't have the patience for this. Within the last twenty-four hours, she must have prayed over four hundred times and was still asking for the Lord's mercy on her child. Her stress level was at an all-time high and it wasn't hard to tell from looking into her bloodshot eyes. She watched the frenzy and chaos behind the window of the receptionist desk in the ER. She closed her red eyes and folded her hands together in prayer. Yes, she was told her son would pull through, but she still wanted to rectify this situation.

"Lord Jesus, please be receptive to my cries. I know I have a rebellious son and I know You know, Lord, he's all I have. But I pray that You allow him a rebirth. In Your name, oh Heavenly

Father. Amen," she spoke silently once more to the man above with her trembling voice. She opened her eyes and was surprised to see a doctor standing in front of her with two police officers.

"Oh, my," she said, startled.

"Uh, excuse me ma'am. I didn't want to bother you while you were praying, but these two officers would like to ask you a few questions…if you don't mind," the doctor asked her as he tried to play mediator but what he should have done was stick to his practice of healing people. If her nerves weren't already shot from her son being beaten and shot, now she was about to be harassed by some cops. She looked from the doctor to the police.

Then she took a deep breath and had a question of her own.

"Please tell me you found the person or people that did this to my son because he's in there bleeding and fighting for his life," she spoke with pride using the last little strength she could muster. The doctor and two police officers looked at the forty-year-old mother with her red teary eyes and her hair all over her head trying to be proud under the circumstances and not crumble under the massive pressure. As they were being observant all three of them noticed that she was alone in the waiting room. Then one of the officers took it upon himself to speak.

"Hmmm, no ma'am we haven't found the person or people. That's why we are here. We have no clue what happened. We have asked the kids who we caught running out the house where your son and his girlfriend was shot and beaten up and whatever they saw, believe me, they're taking it to their graves with them. What-ever they saw must have impacted their ability to talk because they won't say a word," the police officer said.

She looked at him. Then he continued.

"We know this is hard for you, but your son has been in trou-ble before. We looked him up in our database and he's had several arrests and he's currently on parole for a weapons conviction," the officer said to the woman, as if her son's criminal background de-valued his life and the case they were working on. She knew her spiritual well-being could only stand so much before she split, and it was about to break with the next shit he was about to say.

"Is your son in a gang? Did he have any beefs?" the officer asked.

She looked deep into their faces and saw no signs of concern; her sanctity was gone and her salvation was lost.

"If y'all don't get tha fuck out my muthafuckin' face until y'all come and tell me who the bitch niggas is that did this to my son!" she snapped out and stormed out the waiting room down the hall-way and into the room where her son was trying to reclaim his life. The police stood there with the doctor and conversed.

"Hey Doc, what does the dumb bitch want us to do? Huh? This is what happens when they don't watch their children," one officer said with cockiness. The doctor looked as if he wanted to remove himself from the room, but he didn't address the officer's derogatory comments. The doctor bundled his disgust and began to discuss the other crime scene patients.

"Hmm, if you officers will follow me down this way. The other victim is being heavily watched and is under sedation. She's going to need therapy whenever she wakes up. I'm afraid she will never look the same. Almost every bone in her face was either broken or shattered to pieces. She was very fortunate that we could put the few teeth you guys found back in her mouth," the doctor informed them of the girl's physical condition with a nasty taste in his mouth. Both police looked at each other then they began to talk at the same time.

"Doctor…"

"Doc," then one paused so the other could speak.

"Doc so she's not going to be able to tell us anything?" The doctor stopped in his tracks.

"You guys must not have heard the kind of trauma this young girl has been through? She won't be able to do anything for months and here is why," the doctor said as he opened the door to the girl's hospital room. Both of the officers stomachs dropped to the floor when they laid eyes on what the doctor pointed to them in the room.

"Oh shit," one officer whispered, as the other was at a loss for words. The doctor saw them swallow hard as their Adam's apples move up and down in their throats. He knew it was hard for them to look through the door at what was supposed to resemble a girl.

"Yes, as I was saying, she's going to need to speak to a psychologist first before she talks with the police. And that's if she can remember anything at all," the doctor said, feeling a little nauseous as well. He took his hand off the door, so it would close by itself.

"Aye, Doc, why isn't any of the girl's family here?" one of the officers asked. The room they had just looked in was empty. As the doctor was about to answer the question, a nurse walked past the three men.

"Excuse me gentlemen," she said politely while opening the door to check on the girl whose head was almost the same size as the pillow she laid on. The policemen's eyes couldn't help but to peer into the room one more time.

"Shit."

"Doctor with her head that huge… you know what, never mind," one of the officers declined to speak on his curiosity about the medical wonders behind the door they were standing in front of and went back to his twenty questions about the girl's family and why she was lying on her deathbed all alone.

"Uh, yeah, Doc. You were saying…her family is where?"

"Well guys that's an easy question to answer but also an unfortunate one, too," the doctor said leaving them hanging out on a limb and giving them a look of disappointment.

"Well Doc, spit it out for Christ's sake," the other officer said with annoyance in his voice and body language. The doctor wasn't moved one bit, but he answered the question anyhow.

"This girl's family had to leave her, so they could attend a funeral today. They had a relative murdered, a nine-year-old kid. Does that answer the question for your investigation, Officer? If you two will excuse me. I must be going now because my nurse has arrived," the doctor said, walking off, not waiting on a reply or permission to leave.

In the hospital room numbered four-five-six-one the vertical blinds were closed shut, and the lights in the room were turned off. The room was only illuminated by the electronically operated machines keeping her son's life intact. As much as it hurt her soul, Cap's mother sat next to his hospital bed in the darkness. She was a woman of faith, and she knew this situation was nothing but her faith being tested.

Although her son walked in darkness, she prayed every night that one day he would change his life and get it right, so he could walk in the light. In that dimly lit hospital room, her son laid there unconscious in the hospital bed with his head the size of a watermelon and his arm almost torn off at the shoulder. An internal warfare was taking place. Her son's soul was up in the air. The angels and demons hovered over him in battle, and the winner was going to take all. Cap's mother relaxed in her chair and closed her eyes so she could get a little rest. She was going to let her God handle the rest.

"Where, aah-ooo." Cap's mother jumped up out the chair hearing her child's voice. Even in his darkest moment, she wanted him to know she would always be by his side

"Shh-shh…don't talk. Just rest baby, I'm here with you."

"Ahh-Mama…where am I?" Cap asked. Even though he couldn't see her, he knew the warm and loving voice of his mother.

"You're gonna be alright. Okay? Just get some rest baby. I'll be right back. I'm going to get the doctor," she told him as she held his hand tightly inside of hers.

"I can't feel nothing, Mama."

"Shh-shh, I'll be right back baby," she said and let his hand go so she could get the doctor. Cap's mother exited the dark hospital room and as soon as the door closed, she fell to her knees in the hallway and broke out into tears.

The police had no new leads and had decided to leave. The doctor was walking out of the girl's hospital room when he saw Cap's mother in the hallway down on her knees crying. His heart pace sped up and he raced down the hall to her aid.

"Ma'am what's wrong…has he stopped breathing?" he asked Cap's mother but she didn't answer. She was overwhelmed with joy and couldn't hear anything the doctor was asking her. He left her there and ran to the nurse's station.

"Quick, I need you guys! I think we've lost a patient!" the doctor yelled.

Every nurse in the vicinity instantly left their seats and ran with the doctor. They all flew past Cap's crying mother on the floor, burst in his hospital room and flicked on the lights.

"Ahh shit. Cut off the lights. It's hurting my head," Cap groaned in pain. The doctor and every nurse with him stood there confused. Their adrenaline was pumping, and they were breathing hard. The doctor stood in the middle of all the nurses with an embarrassed look written all over his face.

"Okay, uh everybody out," he ordered. They all went out into the hallway to comfort the emotionally drained mother.

"Ma'am, ma'am your son is back." The team of nurses and overreacting doctor helped Cap's mother up from the floor. What were perceived as tears of sadness were only tears of joy. Her prayers had been answered and now she had her son back.

On his behalf people were being laid to rest and the others who came across his path were nearly coming close. Outside his bedroom window in the dead middle of winter, an extremely long line of cars drove slowly in a funeral possession passing by his grandma's house. See, Rockford wasn't a city of skyscrapers, it was a city known for scraping brain fragmentation off the street. Unaware of the new pistol he had confiscated and was now underneath his pillow, Hope was now engraving his name in criminal history.

He laid tossing around in his bed, while the past came back to revisit him in his sleep, not allowing him to rest. His mind was overcome with hallucinations due to the recent homicides, and the truth be told, Hope was fighting with what he'd done and now he had to accept what he had become. In a fraction of time, he had left behind crime scenes only told to rookie officers to scare them on their first day at the job. Although he wasn't known for the murders, he was about to be known for how he was kicking it last night at the card party. And so begins the bullshit.

Chapter Six

Like a baptism, folks had to go to the barbershop to get blessed with a haircut in order to keep their glamour together, so they could feel righteous. Hair was being cut and conductive business was being handled. Bets were being placed at the pool table by customers waiting to get a haircut.

"Rack'em up."

The barber shop was packed wall to wall. In the waiting area, every seat was occupied. People were walking in just to see how long the wait would be. The hustlers weren't going to hear nothing about waiting. For them to wait wasn't in the hustler's code. They couldn't afford to just be sitting around a barbershop waiting on one haircut. There was money to be made. So, when they came in, it was a custom that they pay for two haircuts. The person next to get in the chair, and theirs, plus a tip for the barber. That's how it went, that's how it was done. A hustler always moved by money.

The first seat was about to come open. The barber had just finished up with a customer's head.

"Who's next?" the barber asked, dusting off his chair. As he walked through the door, his timing was perfect. A little boy was getting up out his chair so he could get a haircut and was stopped in his tracks.

"Whoa! Whoa!" Wiggles said.

"Next?" the barber said.

"I got next. Slow down Shorty sit back and get a free haircut little man. You can save up a lil' money and getcha's ah happy meal or somethin'," Wiggles said, budging the line and sitting right down in the barber chair. The little boy looked like he was in desperate need of a haircut and appeared confused.

"My momma said I gotta get a haircut," the little boy said, trying to follow his mom's orders so he wouldn't get an ass whipping.

"Nah, Shorty be cool. Come here," Wiggles said to him, and the kid approached cautiously. "Huh, take this and go sit back down," Wiggles spoke with a bankroll in his hand after peeling off a twenty-dollar bill and handing it to the little fella. The little boy's eyes got big, and his smile grew from ear to ear. He shook his little head up and down.

"Okay, cool," he said and the whole barbershop went up in laughter at his little remark. The little boy pulled out his haircut money his mother gave him and wrapped the twenty-dollar bill on top to make it look like a real bankroll. Then he went back to his seat and began to wait once more on a haircut. His little eyes watched Wiggles being prepared for a haircut with admiration. His little ears were listening to every word coming out of Wiggles' mouth; he and everybody else in the barbershop.

"My man! Wiggles, when they let you out, huh? Whatcha been into baby?" the old school player sitting in the shop asked Wiggles.

"Awe, man, Old School, you know how I move. I'm in and out. I'm here, I'm there, ya dig?" Wiggles said, while the barber was moving the clippers across his head, hair falling to the floor. The player laughed at Wiggles' response because Wiggles reminded him of himself when he was in his youth.

"Yeah, yeah, I can dig it. So, you been cool, huh? I tell a muthafucka like this, play the game for what it's worth. These young cats is falling flat, ya dig...dropping like flies," the old school player said and lit a cigarette.

Wiggles sat in the barber chair as his eyes scanned the room. He was taking inventory of how many snakes were in the room. He quickly caught a few familiar faces in the crowd with glossy eyes, but they were no threat.

"Old School you ain't said nothing. I saw a nigga and his bitch get that ass rushed last night. Ahhh, man, y'all don't hear me. This nigga named Hope, yeah...I think that's his name. Anyway, man this nigga never cared." The little boy sitting in the chair waiting to get his haircut was becoming intoxicated by the way Wiggles moved and talked, and he continued to analyze him.

"I mean this nigga was kicking ass all ova' the place and when I say all ova' the place I mean all ova' the place. I had to get out of his way," Wiggles said, and everybody laughed.

"Huh, Wiggles, you had to get out of his way?" the barber said, because he had to stop and laugh.

"Yeah, man, I'm not bullshittin'. Y'all laughing and shit but that was serious," Wiggles told them all, with a look of concern because he didn't feel they really understood where he was coming from. The whole reason he was bringing this up was because he was trying to give everybody a warning just in case they came across that nigga's path but yet they were all in there laughing.

"Man, he was in there kicking muthafucka's all in they face. Yeah. Even after they were out cold. Man, I'm telling ya."

"Aye, Wiggles did he shoot ah muthafucka, too?" one of the other customers asked.

"Yep," Wiggles replied and looked in the mirror to see how good of a job the barber was doing. Then people began to break off into their own conversations mumbling to each other. That's when Wiggles knew shit was starting to register.

"Wiggles, man what you doing 'round that shit baby?" the old school player asked him, not that he really wanted to know but it was more of a question to bring an awareness.

"Old School I wasn't in there for that. I was in there trying to lay this meat in something. Ya feel me, School?" Wiggles said laughing. Old School laughed, too.

"Ha, ha! So, did you meet a bitch mane?" Wiggles gave Old School a look that gave him the answer. Wiggles looked out the window of the barbershop and saw his girl about to walk in.

"Aye, School, check this. God-damnit, this is what I was on last night before that bullshit happened," Wiggles told him as she walked in the building. Every eye in the room watched as she walked in. That's how good she was looking. Her cinnamon brown skin tone was looking so sweet. Wiggles thought he'd seen the little boy sitting in the waiting chair licking his lips at her. She wore her makeup just right and her pants were skintight showing the imprint of her vagina *and* her ass was huge. The short black fur coat couldn't hold back her big breast. She wore her hair parted down the middle, sporting two braids going to the back and hanging down her back.

"Say man, don't fuck my head up looking at my lady friend," Wiggles said to the barber. Everybody laughed.

"Aye, Ke-Ke you got these niggas in here with valentine hearts in their eyes," he said looking back in the mirror at himself to make sure the barber didn't fuck him up for real. She stood in the middle of the barbershop looking so serious while chewing her gum and her glossy lips shined.

"You almost done? Don't you still want to go to the mall?" she asked him. Wiggles looked in the mirror again.

"Yeah, almost. Go wait in the car and I'll be out in a minute." She spun around like a model, and everybody watched her ass as she passed by their way and walked out the door. Old School jumped up from his seat feeling a slight erection in his pants and went to the window so he could see more.

"Aye, Wiggles, I ain't no sucker and I ain't no square but I don't care. I would have been in there ducking bullets last night, too, trying to get to that ass mane!" he told Wiggles and the whole barbershop went to laughing at Old School's statement. Wiggles kept his cool as the barber was finishing up on his head.

"Aye, man, School, she ain't on shit. She's ah eater." Old School looked at him crazy.

"Nigga she ain't fat," he scolded Wiggles.

"Nah, Old School that ain't what that mean. When I say she's ah eater, I mean she eats dick for breakfast, lunch, and dinner. Shit I'm about to drive to the mall and give her a snack on the way out there," Wiggles enlightened Old School about the new slang and things. Old School grabbed his crotch and continued to watch Ke-Ke's thick ass walk to her car.

"Mmm-mmm, dick for breakfast, lunch, and dinner? Ah eater, huh? I think I'm gonna need me one of dem," he declared. Then under his breath he repeated himself, "Ah e-a-t-e-r, breakfast, lunch, and dinner." Old School shook it off and walked outside and lit up another square. Then he stood in front of the barber shop to see if he could find an eater for himself to feed.

The barber removed the hair cape from around Wiggles' neck.

"A'ight, you good, my man?" the barber said, dusting the excess hair off his clothes. Wiggles jumped out the barber chair and walked up to a mirror. He wanted to do a thorough inspection of his hair, just to make sure everything was everything.

"Aye, shorty, I'm cool?" Wiggles asked the little boy he'd budged in line for a haircut. The little boy smiled.

"Yep, you cool," the little boy replied. Wiggles reached in his pocket and pulled out the large bankroll.

"Okay cool," Wiggles said, handing the barber a twenty-dollar bill stained with blood.

"What tha fuck is this?" the barber asked looking astonished. Wiggles kept it moving like he hadn't heard a word the barber said.

"C'mon shorty, you better hurry up before somebody takes your turn again," Wiggles said to the little boy putting the clippers on him. The little boy leaped from his seat, flew across the floor and jumped in the barber chair happy. The barber looked down at the little boy's hair and rolled his eyes. The kid's hair looked like it had been neglected for months. His hair was extra nappy and was covered with white lint balls. Wiggles used the diversion to slide out the door. Soon as he stepped out the door, Wiggles saw Old School talking with a lit cigarette between his lips. The cigarette was moving up and down as he spoke.

"Yeah, yeah, so dig right. Let me get you out this cold weather and feed you baby. You hungry? I know you like to eat. Don't you?"

Wiggles overheard a small portion of the game Old School was running on some female. Wiggles walked past shaking his head because he saw the woman and Old School begin to leave together from in front of the barbershop. Wiggles couldn't help himself. He had to know where Old School was going with the lady. So, he put both hands up to his mouth and yelled, "Old School! Where are you going?"

Old School had his arm wrapped around the woman. He didn't stop walking, but he looked back. "I'm taking baby to a buffet so she can eat all she can eat!" Old School yelled back to Wiggles and continued to lead the way.

"Man, School is a muhfucka." Wiggles laughed to himself and opened the door to Ke-Ke's car. She was sitting in the passenger seat waiting on Wiggles. He hopped in the car, and she looked at him licking her lips.

"You got something for me?" Ke-Ke asked him with a seductive tone in her voice. He put the car in gear, and she was gearing up to drive down on him as she began to unzip his pants.

Meanwhile back in the barbershop the talking had started.

"He said Hope?"

"Yeah, he said Hope."

"Ain't that…"

Chapter Seven

The crying turned into hostility. They would forever be enslaved to his wickedness. He had distributed death and great bodily harm as punishment for getting out of line with him. He would not be made a mockery of. The streets weren't going to stomach the extreme pressure he was about to bear down. Like a volcano, something on the inside of him had erupted. And to protect himself and his interests, he was going to keep leaving niggas horizontal and transported to the cemetery, no matter how many families had to weep on his behalf.

By the time Hope awaken from his nightmares, one open casket had been closed. The nine-year-old boy's family had buried and laid him to rest. Hope was laying all his burdens down. The first-person Hope had ever killed was now officially rotting underground. As for the rest of them, there was one more old rotten nigga in a few days about to be put to rest, Hope's second murder victim named Slim Pickens.

Then with great bodily harm, the goofball named Cap and his girlfriend with the extremely swollen head and facial reconstruction laid on bed rest in the hospital clinging onto their little lives.

Far as he knew, there were crickets on his name, and it better had stayed that way. There was no reason for anyone to be speaking on his business. Hope sat up and rubbed his hand over his face and then stretched out his arms.

"Damn, what time is it?" he asked himself while hopping off the bed. Hope slowly walked over to his bedroom window and peeped through the white mini blinds.

"What's popping outside this bitch?" he said as his eyes scanned the area so the streets could reveal themselves to him. Through the frosty window in the cold weather, Hope could see that the day had slipped away, and the night had fell on him. He let the mini blinds go and made-up his mind.

"Ahh, shit. Let's get to it," he told himself, walked to the bathroom and closed the door behind him. While taking a shower, the hot water couldn't cleanse his soul nor wash the blood from his hands. He had caused irreversible damage that had now set off a new chain of events. Hope was letting bullets fly and shells eject, depriving people of their family members. He jumped out the shower fresh and began to get dressed. Due to the cold conditions on the hot streets outside his crib, Hope had to dress accordingly to keep the heat concealed and his body warm.

He slipped his leg into a brand new and crisp pair of long-johns for the first layer of protection. Hope was a well dresser, everything he put on had to match. He removed the price tag from the clothing and slithered into the expensive dark smoky gray sweatsuit made from a soft and fine fabric. To make sure he was standing on business, Hope put on a fresh pair of dark smokey gray suede cloth boots to give himself the trickle-down effect.

He had to get a full view of the bigger picture. So, he strolled over to a full-length mirror which hung on his grandma's wall. He smiled, as he looked himself up and down.

"Yeah, gotta stay on fleek," Hope boasted in the mirror, he was impressed with his own self-image. Who was going to love Hope like Hope? Nobody. Then a quick image of the dying junkie coughing on his own blood flashed across the mirror.

"Huh?" Hope jumped back startled. See killing was easy phys-ically, but mentally it was hard. The sounds, smells, feelings, and faces would never perish from memory. It was like a souvenir, a memento from death, so began the poltergeist.

As quick as the dying image of the junkie came, it was gone even faster. Hope stared in the mirror at the still healing scar en-graved across his throat. He did not know that he also had a men-tal scar engraved across his mind. Hope had been born and raised in Illinois, but he now was truly ill.

"Fuck this, I ain't tweakin'. I'm out," Hope grilled himself, then turned around and spun off from the mirror. Hope grabbed the smokey gray leather designer coat out of his closet and put it on. He reached in the right-side coat pocket and pulled out a black skull cap. Well, to the naked eye it appeared to be a black skull but in reality when it was fully pulled down over his face, the black skull cap was really a ski mask rolled up. He put it on the top of his head and wore it stylishly. Hope was fresh and geared up, now it was time for him to strap up. He grabbed the new .40 caliber pistol from underneath his pillow, the one he'd disarmed from Cap. He checked the chamber to make sure there was still one in the head.

"Mmmm-hmm," he said, and placed it on his hip inside the coat. Then he grabbed the other two guns and placed them where he felt necessary on his person. Hope stopped for a moment to see if he could hear his grandma rummaging about throughout the house, but it was silent like the Fifth Amendment. Hope walked through the empty home not looking at the pictures of the broken family hanging on the wall. He made his way in the kitchen and didn't even check the refrigerator. He just bailed out the back door. Tonight was a new night for him and something had to shake.

He looked up to the sky and saw a starlit night. It looks so peaceful up there to him and that was something he knew he would never have. Hope took a deep breath so the sharp cold air of the night could bless his lungs. Although he could never have peace, he was alive, and for whatever reason it was worth, Hope was going to make sure he'd stayed that way. Hope took a step off his back porch, began to crunch through the snow in his backyard and merge into the dark alley. He started walking in the trails left behind from other people not wanting to create any new foot traffic.

The familiar sounds of the night serenaded his ears. He walked alongside fences where dogs rushed the gate growling and barking at him. Up ahead the flames could be seen growing from a steel barrel. Loud arguing and hollering came from junkies in combat over who was going to be the next person up to bat for a swing. In the distance, maybe a few blocks West, Hope could hear gunshots being let off. He continued to walk the path and was stopped by a person he knew.

"And there was Hope," the man said greeting him in his own fashion.

"Old School, What's up my dude? What you need?" Hope asked and pulled out his sack of goodies. Old School handed Hope an undisclosed amount of money.

"Okay cool," Hope told him and gave Old School the good stuff. Hope finished his business and was about to walk off when Old School stopped him.

"Yeah, Hope we cool, but umm—"

"But what! Old School?" Hope said with his face all frowned up.

"Ummm, your name ringin' baby. This kat named Wiggles came in the barbershop talking a whole mutha fuckin' lot. Frontin' off your move. Hey, you know me, how you handle your business, is how you handle your business, but the nigga Wiggles is morally out-a-pocket. Puttin' ya business on blast in the barbershop like that. Man, dig what I'm sayin'? Ain't no telling where that information 'done landed by now. All's I'm sayin' is be cool and do what you gotta do. You know, you like family to me, may your mother and brother rest in peace."

Hope's face was tight, and his heart was pounding hard. It wasn't hard to tell that something bad was going to happen and Old School knew Wiggles was in big trouble.

"Man! Old School this nigga don't even know me, how the fuck he got my name in his mouth like a bitch! Aye, man what the fuck he drivin', huh? Who he be with, huh? Where he be at?" There was a lot of things Hope wanted to know.

"Whoa, Hope I don't know all that, but earlier today that nigga was with some bitch driving her car. I think he said her name was Ke-Ke or some dumb shit like that. Yeah, yeah, Ke-Ke that's what it was," he told Hope and lit a cigarette. "Yeah Ke-Ke," Old School repeated.

"Ke-Ke! He fuckin' with Ke-Ke? Okay, okay, I know exactly what car he's in. I'm gone. Matter-fact huh, take these." Hope blessed Old School with a few more goodies for his full corroboration and stormed off. Old School walked back towards the fire and joined the congregation of junkies arguing.

"Hey baby look what I got. You can come with me, but you gotta be ah eater." Old School flashed what he had in his hand to a dope fiend female, and she quickly walked off with him.

After just hearing the disturbing news, Hope couldn't even walk or think straight. Wherever and whenever he laid eyes on Wiggles it was going to be a real muthafuckin' disturbance.

"Why the fuck he talking about me? What I do to him, huh? Huh, what I do to him? No, what I'm gonna do to his ass though!" Hope was walking and talking to himself, trying to figure out the reason he was going to lay this nigga down. "Ke-Ke not for real, that bitch is a straight undercover eater. I should pop that bitch, too. Just for letting that nigga drive her car and knowin' he's speakin' on my name." Hope's talking turned into growling and his anger was turning into insanity, "Muthafuckas! Whew, I can't wait!" he yelled up to the sky with all his might.

But just like Hope was feeling at that exact moment, it was some niggas out there riding around feeling the same way about him and on his ass for the shit that he had done last night at the card game. All the chit-chat in the barbershop caught some shark's attention at the pool table.

Let's talk about real killers, let's talk about a muthafucka who would kill you for a little nothing, so just imagine what they were going to do over a loved one. On his account a lot of bodies were left lying around waiting to be found by the police and be pronounced dead on arrival.

The graveyards across the city were indebted to him. It definitely wasn't a good sign if he had you on his mind, and the only thing he could think about was finding him some *Hope.*

The nigga looking for Hope was named Maytag. There was no question about how crazy this nigga was. The crazy thing about it, his name would tell you everything you needed to know about him. What kind of person would call himself Maytag?

The kind of person who may leave your ass dead with a tag on your toe. Hence the name Maytag was derived from people's lips. The folklore surrounding his name was nothing compared to his hideous outward appearance. He had a significant look considering his left eye had been cut out due to an act of violence and his face was all diced and sliced the fuck up. It was said that back in the day, he came across a nigga way, way crazier than him, named Ricardo. It happened when they were shorties. Some bull shit happened to where Ricardo took his eye out with a straight razor and cut his face up like a fish filet. Leaving him trying to hold his shit together, while running in front of a police car almost getting hit. Now whether it's true or not, who knows. The truth is, people will always talk and find a way to fabricate the truth, but whatever happened back in the day, it was an eye opener for him because he was a killer now, and no matter how repulsive he looked, it was best to keep your opinions to yourself.

After leaving the barbershop, playing pool, and hearing his own had been kicked around at a party, Maytag flew to the hospital to have his heartbroken. He walked in the hospital room and couldn't even recognize what used to be his beautiful little princess. His only daughter, his only child looked like some kind of monster. His stomach had turned into knots when he saw her head. Right then and there it was already set in stone. He was going to kill Hope, *Joy*, and whoever else has something to do with the permanent disfigurement of his daughter. It hurt him so much that he couldn't bear the sight of her and took off.

Maytag hit the streets on real business, family business, nothing on this ride or in the car was artificial. It was real, definitely what he just saw. He was in search of Hope. Cutting corners in the night, the strong offensive smell of the burning leaf in the car was a taboo to the nose and a stinger to the eyes. Maytag was riding high. On his ride he was being accompanied with bad company. It was accustomed that birds of a feather flock together. Ducked low with the passenger seat laid back, there was another accomplished killer moving with the motive of murder on his mind.

Maytag inhaled the strong fumes from the burning leaf and promptly passed the motivation over to his cut throat partner named Finito. Finito was a silent shooter, his thought process was kind of off, a lot of things didn't really register to him. Finito took the motivation Maytag had passed to him, put it up to his lips and inhaled it three real quick times.

He coughed and passed it right back. Finito's blood shot eyes stared out the passenger side window as he remained hidden under a black hoodie, pulled over his head. He kept what little focus he had on the matter at hand. Not one word was said in the car.

It was a feeling of great anticipation and Maytag was loving it all. Riding around with a Draco sitting in his lap. He seemed to be under some hypnosis of anger. He just couldn't wait to knock Hope off with it.

Maytag was so anxious; he could already feel the excitement of just laying his eye on Hope. His dirty palms were sweaty as he guided the chrome and wood customized steering wheel of the super clean two tone green and light-green, old school 1977 four door Pontiac Bonneville Brougham with 400V8 motor. Running the right way and looking extremely beautiful due to its rarity the mirror like twenty-four-inch customized chrome rims were glaring from the street lights. It was just a small indicator that the car would run on the side of anything. The silence was broken.

"Yo, yo, what's, what's, that right there?" Finito questioned his sight. Maytag quickly zoomed in on the question Finito threw in the air. He saw a boy walking out the dark towards one of the infamous gas stations known for yellow tape and bullets flying for recreation.

"I don't know, we about to see though," Maytag let him know and whipped the two-tone green Bonneville into the gas station parking lot.

Ahead of the boy, the car pulled up and parked right in front of the gas station door. They both grabbed their guns and watched him entering the parking lot.

"That's him, huh, is it? C'mon man is that him?" Finito eagerly wanted to know with his fingers itchy on the trigger as he deeply inhaled some more motivation. Still holding his breath, a cloud of smoke came from his mouth and nose. Finito asked again in a strained voice.

"Is that the nigga?" He was starting to lift his gun. "Huh, is that him man?"

"Hold on. Here this muthafucka come now," Maytag said lifting his gun up slightly and at the same time rolling down the car window.

Walking up to the gas station, the boy had peeped something foxy. He continued to walk but right before he could get five feet to the door, he could see a window roll down and a thick cloud of smoke come from the green, old-school car parked right in front of the door where he had to go into the gas station.

"Man," he said still investigating the situation. He could smell that shit they were smoking and with the strong odor came a strong overwhelming feeling. His street smarts began to kick in and he instantly knew that smoke was for him.

He had real trouble in front of him, and out of the cloud of smoke coming from the car, he could hear someone call out, "Aye, shorty."

Chapter Eight

Privileged and pleasured, and as perplexing as it may sound, Wiggles was exhausted from the privilege of receiving pleasure coming from some prestigious head. He was being fully drained and could no longer maintain his composure. From the driver's seat, Ke-Ke smiled at her work.

"Baby, you cool over there?" she asked, while giggling a little bit from the driver's seat. Wiggles had fell back from behind the wheel because of the way she had dropped knowledge in his lap. The feeling had him about to do something dumb, like crash the car. Her confidence was at an all-time high and his energy level was at an all-time low.

"Why are you fucking with me, huh?" he asked from the passenger's seat stretched out with his pants still unzipped and his limp joint hanging out. She giggled again, reached over in Wiggles' lap and laid a hand on him.

"Is this mine baby?" Ke-Ke asked, wanting to know about her membership. One hand was maneuvering the Chevrolet Equinox down the street, as her other hand was slowly manipulating his manhood. Ke-Ke's eyes stayed focused on the road and her hands stayed focused on him. She could tell from what she was doing that it was feeling sensational to him by the way he was swelling up. "Huh, is this mine, boy?" She moaned and continued to promote his and her membership. Wiggles was already worn out. So, he sat in the passenger seat at a disadvantage. As she handled him, Ke-Ke's feminine moans made Wiggles start feeling some obligations to her.

"Uh, what you talkin' 'bout, I just got out," he protested, which provoked her to press down harder on him. "Damn Ke-Ke, shit!" he said, looking over at her concentrating on the road and biting down on her lip, trying to compel him into becoming hers.

To him this was crazy, he was fresh out. The Chevrolet Equinox came to a stop at the red light. There was traffic all around, some cars stopped on the side and behind them. Ke-Ke took that brief intermission, leaned over and used her lips like a lasso.

"Oh, shit girl!" he literally cried out. Wiggles could feel himself descend her throat and the walls of her mouth was so warm and juicy, that he forgot everything he stood for. It was a wrap. She was thirsty and for him there was no more self-control. The lights turned green, and cars were honking their horns, impatiently waiting for them to go. Ke-Ke acted as if she hadn't heard a thing and Wiggles couldn't hear a thing because she was overbearing him. Cars angrily swung around them almost side-swiping the Chevy. Wiggles was living in the moment and couldn't have cared less. Ke-Ke's head was repeatedly moving up and down in his lap. He took his hand and pressed down on the back of her head. There was no resistance from her and at that moment Ke-Ke's precious mouth unmistakably had Wiggles separating himself from his seeds again.

"Ahhh," he moaned sentimentally. With her head still down in his lap and her mouth full, Ke-Ke asked again.

"Is this mine, Wiggles?" He had been crippled and the only thing to do was to give Ke-Ke what she wanted. He took a deep breath and gave her an answer. It was a go.

"Ya got me, yeah this dick yours," he told Ke-Ke, rubbing the back of her head. "It's yours," he reassured her. The traffic lights had turned back red. Ke-Ke was satisfied with his vibes and after swallowing the fruits of life, she wiped her mouth and raised her head high. The lights turned green, and they drove off.

"I need something to drink, you want anything?" she asked Wiggles and pulled the red Chevrolet Equinox into the parking lot of her favorite gas station. Ke-Ke's eyes locked on a two-tone, green, old school 1977 Bonneville sitting lazy on chrome, looking fascinating under the lights in the parking lot. She had already made her mind up; she was getting out the car and going in to pay for whatever they wanted.

On the passenger side was a whole different story though. Unaware he had been marked for death, Wiggles was still marveling over Ke-Ke's phenomenal mouthpiece and feeling pretty good about himself. Today had been a damn good day considering he'd only been out of juvenile prison for two days. She pulled up right next to the flashy old school car. She parked and turned on the interior lights and began digging in her Gucci purse. Ke-Ke began humming to the music playing on her radio. Wiggles was totally oblivious to where they were until he sat up and started looking around.

"What the fuck is you doing here?" he barked at her. Ke-Ke flinched and then straightened her posture. She squinted her sexy eyes and gave Wiggles a serious stare down, but he wasn't paying that little shit no attention. He knew he was somewhere he didn't need to be without some fireworks. This shit was bigger than Nino Brown, he was out of pocket. Wiggles was sitting at the hottest place in Rockford, Illinois in the passenger seat of a known THOT's car with his pants unzipped and his dick hanging out, with no gun.

"Nigga I just told you I was thirsty and I wanted something to drink. Don't you remember me just asking you did you want something, no matter of fact, I said *anything*. Did you want anything?" she gave him a small recap of what she said to him only moments earlier. Still, Wiggles wasn't listening to anything she was talking about. His eyes were examining his current situation and calculating the extreme danger he was in. This wasn't a place known for misdemeanors, it was known for niggas getting massacred. Ke-Ke saw he wasn't paying her any mind.

"Anyway," she said sarcastically and went back to digging in her Gucci purse until she found her lip gloss. Ke-Ke let down the vanity mirror and began to gloss her sexy and oh-so luscious lips.

Wiggles wasn't trying to get injured with his dick hanging out and his pants unzipped, so he quickly put his package up and fixed his pants.

"Damn, what the fuck is you doing. Huh? Get me tha fuck outta here!" He was making his demands and still looking around the area.

"You gotta wait a minute. I'm not leaving here until I get me something to drink!" she yelled at him.

He was getting angry with her, she wanted to play this pussy ass game while jeopardizing his safety. Wiggles kept looking over her shoulder at the car sitting in a cloud of smoke on some bullshit. He could see some real foxy business going on over there. Through the smoky windows of the Bonneville, Wiggles could see a nigga wearing a black hoodie in the passenger seat looking jumpy, like he was about to get ready to shoot somebody. He looked back to see what had dude in the Bonneville so jumpy. It was a boy outside walking up to the gas station who was seeing the exact same thing, but the boy walking knew some shit was about to go down, and the smoke was for him.

"Do you want anything, Wiggles?" Ke-Ke asked him again while putting the lip gloss back in her purse and shutting off the interior light.

"Bitch!" he yelled, "I want you to get me tha fuck outta here!" that remark pissed Ke-Ke off as she snatched the keys out the ignition, jumped her thick-thighs and big booty-self out the ride and slammed the car door. She threw her ass hard, walking past the Bonneville unaware that those niggas weren't paying her no muthafuckin' attention. They were trying to debate if the boy walking up was Hope or not.

"Man, is that the muthafucka or what? Man, watch out, I'm finna pop this nigga. I don't give ah fuck if it's Hope or not!"

And it wasn't. The boy walking up to the gas station was not Hope, because Hope was just about to cross the busy street leading up to the gas station, from the opposite direction when he became geeked at seeing Ke-Ke's car parked up there. The interior light was shining down on who he was looking for. Hope quickly ran out of sight and got low. Then for some strange reason, Hope was watching the two sitting in the old school Bonneville on some boy's heels, but it didn't have shit to do with him. He was on Wiggles' ass for all that phat mouthing in the barbershop earlier that day.

"I got you now," Hope said, as he pulled the black ski mask down over his face and kept repeating to himself, "I got your ass right now." Hope pulled out his FN-Five-SeveN. He took the clip out and checked it to make sure it was full. He put it back in and then checked the chamber. He had one in the hole ready to go. His hot breath blew through the black ski mask and disappeared into the night. Hope held the gun with both hands for better accuracy and ran across the street.

BLOCKA! BLOCKA!

Hope let the bullets rain down on everybody in the gas station parking lot. He never cared. BLOCKA! BLOCKA! BLOCKA! BLOCKA! BLOCKA! BLOCKA!

"Bitch ass. Got my name in your mouth," Hope said, still letting his gun blow.

BLOCKA! BLOCKA! BLOCKA! BLOCKA! BLOCKA! BLOCKA! BLOCKA! BLOCKA! BLOCKA! BLOCKA! BLOCKA! CLICK!

Shell casings fell out the FN-Five-SeveN chamber until the sun came up.

It was morning and Hope had the gas station looking like a foreign land. It resembled a war zone in Afghanistan. The news camera zoomed in on the black body bag lying on the ground near the passenger side of a bullet riddled Bonneville sitting on three flats. Then the news camera zoomed in on a windowless, bullet riddled, red Chevrolet Equinox which also sat on flat tires. Dark dried-up blood from the injured victims was seen on the seats and all over the ground at the gas station's parking lot. A young redhead female news reporter stood in front of the gas station's wall, where the bullets had ripped through it and left pebbles on the ground.

"As you can see, the gunshots went through the gas station's wall, leaving large peep holes, where I can currently see a brave customer making a purchase at the cash register," she said, leaning over peeping through one of the large bullet holes in the wall. Then she gazed back into the camera with the news station logo microphone in her hand and continued to give the viewers key details on last night's shooting.

"One man is dead, two other men critically wounded, and a woman was lucky enough to have only been grazed in the leg during the deadly rainstorm of bullets. That's all from here, now switching over to the newsroom."

Hope stood up from the couch he was on and left his grandma sitting there watching the rest of the news.

"Grandma, I'm finna go back to sleep. I left you some money on the kitchen table, a'ight?" he told her and walked off to his bedroom. Hope's grandma watched him walk off. Then she looked at the family's pictures hanging on the wall reminiscing back to when times were much happier for them.

Then she heard a knock at the door, so she slowly eased up from the couch. Hope's grandma was a very small old lady, with long whitish grey hair. She wore a few pieces of expensive gold and diamond jewelry to let you know her involvement. She leaned over just a little so she could reach what was under the couch. Hope's grandma strolled over to the door.

CLICK! She cocked that .25 caliber chrome and pearl white handgun.

"Who is it?" she called out. There was a reply from the other side, and she opened the door to let the customer in. "Hey, child. How many bags you want?" Hope's grandma said, as she held the small, beautiful gun at her side.

"Wait, and I know you got my money from last time, yeah, better not come over here trying to shop and ain't got my money you owe me from the last time," she reminded the loyal customer.

"Yeah, I got that, and I need three," the customer said looking at the gun in Hope's grandma's hand and gave her the money.

"Okay, child here you go, and you be careful out there. I saw on the news this morning they shootin' and killin' like crazy. And I don't wanna see you get hurt, okay?" Then she let the customer out the door and locked it. She walked back over to the couch, put the gun up, sat back down and went back to watching the bad news on TV.

Chapter Nine

Even in the streets, no matter how strong a person may feel they are, it's so important to have family and friends in this cold and wicked world. When days get gloomy and grim, when the severe storms are overhead, and the deep waters become troublesome, a person will need someone to help build a bridge to carry them over the heavy load.

The church was almost empty. The polished cherry wood casket sat closed in front of the pulpit. The gunshot wound to his face was unrepairable, so a picture was placed on top of the cherry wood casket to view the subject in the box. Only three people showed up and were in attendance for the junkie's funeral service. His elderly mother dressed in all black attire sat in the front row. She stared at the picture on the casket. Then sitting in the back of the church were two filthy dressed undesirables, they were high as a kite nodding off as they tried to pay their respects to their street comrade. The sharp dressed minister stood at the podium in his red suit and red gator shoes. In the junkie's life, he had burned down every bridge he had ever come across. The minister looked out to the congregation of only a few. This was nothing in comparison to the funeral he did a couple of days ago for the unfortunate nine-year-old boy. Nevertheless, the show must go on, regardless of how large or small the crowd was. He was being paid to preach.

"Black men are dying, and mothers are crying. Unclean needles injecting affliction into the arms of our Black sons. Dope crippling manhood's, leaving the family structure withering away. Men wanting to nod instead of going to get a job. Aww, don't y'all go to sleep on me now, because I'm gonna preach."

The clean minister came around and stepped down from the podium. He walked up to the cherry wood casket and looked at the picture sitting on top of it.

"Right now, there are one million black men sitting in cages, in prisons across this country, because they were tricked to believe in a unique concept. That they got to "slang" to maintain. But the truth is, it's all make-believe. Black men are being made to believe that any form of disrespect is punishable by death. Yet, I say make-believe! Our young Black men are being made to believe that our Black lives are valueless, so they gamble with their life for the value of a dollar and crap out to the streets or prison. We kidnap our own, we rob our own, we batter our own, we shoot our own, we kill our own…look at the mental and physical scars left on our beautiful Black people. We fear our own, look at police statements, it's there, right there in black and white. We tell on our own people and that's not make-believe. Got our Black daughters as soon as they are old enough to walk, dancing to the music, backing that *thang* up in a diaper. C'mon now, I'm gonna preach, don't y'all go to sleep on me now." The minister walked back and forth, in front of the junkie's casket. He was starting to bust a sweat because that's what he was getting paid for.

"Young Black boys receiving mail from jail from their male role-models, so of course, they're gonna follow their daddies to prison and be made to believe this is how life goes. And there's nothing we can do about it, and I say make-believe!" the minister yelled into the microphone he held in his hand. The rumble in his voice was a disturbance to one of the undesirables sitting in the back of the church because he quickly flinched in his nod and scratched the side of his face. The sharp-dressed minister contin-ued with his sermon.

"You can make your kids believe in themselves! You can make your kids believe they are valued. We can be better people by tak-ing the right actions. Look at our Black leaders. They are dressed to impress and talking hot mess on the TV screen, but do you see them in our projects? No, because they made it out and they made a vow to stay out. They have upscaled and won't help the rest pre-vail. Our people are morally being lynched as money takes the new place of Willie Lynch! Let's pray for a new day!" the minister preached.

"Amen!"

"Sho' ya right, Pastor."

"Preach!"

Chapter Ten

The whole community of Rockford had something in common. The news showed night after night the graphic nature of the bloody and deadly violence that had taken place on the city streets. There were people dying that everyone knew. The hospital was full, and the streets were becoming empty. The police were riding on easy street. All the illegal hotspots looked like a desert. Nobody was out walking around because nobody knew who was laying down the pressure, so it was just best to stay out the way.

"Can you believe this, Tom? There is absolutely not a soul out here."

The police officer laughed at his partner, the driver of the blue and white squad car. He was making jokes and laughing it up at the people's fear of getting killed.

"C'mon, take me somewhere so I can get me some donuts. We don't have to worry about anything happening out here tonight. This place is a ghost town," he laughed again.

Chapter Eleven

On an axis the world turns a full 360 degrees in a twenty-four-hour span. And in less than one second, a person's mind can turn inside out from being hurt.

Everybody has a turning point in life. Hope was dripping in sweat with his heart beating out his chest. There was no rest for him as he wrestled with his conscious state during his sleep. Hope tossed and turned in his bed. No matter how long it'd been, a person couldn't forget the pain…forget the pain, pain, pain… In his dream Hope could hear the voices.

"Bitch what's his muthafuckin' name! Huh?" Vic yelled and slam dunked his girlfriend on the hardwood floor making her little body bounce like a basketball. Gabby lost the majority of her wind upon impact. She was a dream girl and too beautiful to be getting physically abused by a towering six-foot five-inch nigga with pure strength. Her yellow toned body bruised where she landed. The one-bedroom apartment was in shambles from him going crazy

over the rumor. Pictures were knocked off the wall. Small glass tables had been shattered from him flipping them over. The black leather furniture was knocked around and in disarray. Their relationship as they knew it was fundamentally over, done, a wrap, finished.

She screamed at the top of her lungs, "Ahhhh! Please stop baby. I don't know—"

Vic slapped Gabby in mid-sentence across her mouth while she was trying to get up, gather and explain herself.

"You fuckin' this nigga and you don't know his muthafuckin' name!" Vic said, demanding a name, he cocked back and gave her a right hook to the eye doing her so wrong. She fell backwards to the floor with her quick swollen shut eyes. Miraculously Gabby didn't lose consciousness. Whispers of her past misdeeds were the reasons she wasn't seeing things clearly.

"How long you been fuckin' this nigga?" Vic grabbed Gabby by her soft, long hair and pulled her up from the floor. The tears poured from her good and bad eye.

"Baby, I didn't mean for it to happen!" Gabby cried out, admitting her guilt. Vic was overtaken by shock and his heart dropped. The man's soul was torn from his body. Her words of guilt stole all the love he had or would ever have for her. Flashes of her sexual behavior started to transmit through his mind. Vic's skin crawled as he began fantasizing about how another man was grabbing Gabby with aggression and clapping her cheeks with

force like he used to. He could see how the next man enjoyed kissing on his girlfriend's perfect, soft breasts and digging deep in her pussy that gushed with every powerful stroke. He cringed when his mind reminded him of the way she sounded when having the world's wettest orgasm.

"Oh, but you let it happen," he confirmed her wrongdoings and slapped Gabby across the face again.

"Ahh, Vic I'm sorry! I'm sorry! Stop hitting me!" she squirmed around, still being held against her will by her hair. All Vic could see was her and another nigga fucking.

"Stop hitting you?" He looked at her like she was crazy. "Okay you want me to stop. A'ight," he said and with a sense of calmness, Vic's hand released her hair and she dropped to the hardwood floor, relieved. Gabby knew he still loved her. She could see his anger leaving his face as sorrow set in. The man broke down crying. A six-foot-five-inch nigga boo hoo-ing like a newborn baby.

There are reasons people build walls around their hearts. It's a thin line that separates love from hate and deception is what cuts it.

"Baby we can fix this," she told him, while getting close to him.

"I know," Vic agreed with his girlfriend. They began to cry together and held each other close.

"I'm so sorry baby," she whispered in his ear.

"I know, I know," he told her. Then he let her go and walked away. "I know."

She could hear him repeating himself. He was out of sight, and she was just glad that he wasn't hitting her anymore and that he'd calmed down. Her friends had warned her that if he ever found out about her cheating he would react this way. Gabby was happy that she got this part out the way because as soon as she healed she was going to fuck and suck all on her new ballin' ass street nigga who she was now in love with. Gabby began smiling at the thought. Gabby started picking up the broken things in her apartment.

"Pathetic," she mumbled to herself, looking in the direction Vic had walked off in. Then suddenly, she heard him coming back, repeating the same thing as before.

"I know," he said as he came around the corner, heated. Gabby looked at the Glock 9 mm. Vic was holding and screamed through the roof. She was shaking like a stripper.

"Bitch, what's his muthafuckin' name? You better tell me or I'ma pop your dumb ass right now," Vic said, pointing the gun in Gabby's face with the hammer cocked back.

"Truth! Truth! His name is Truth!" she told Vic in hopes that he wouldn't push her shit back.

Sitting at the kitchen table, Hope and his older brother Truth were playing a card game called Casino. They were trying to tune out noises of their grandma and mom's arguing. Every time it was *the same ol' shit. Out of nowhere Hope and Truth's mama would show up wanting some money for her habit. She loved her kids, but dope had its foot standing on her neck and wouldn't let up. Back in the day, there was a time their mother was the prettiest woman in town. But all that changed when she had been tricked into introducing the dope into her life. She no longer talked or walked the same.*

"Mama I'm in pain, just give me the god-damn money so I can go."

"What about your kids? They haven't seen you in weeks," Hope's grandma told his momma.

"I know, give me some money so I can get well, and I'll be back to cook y'all a big dinner," Hope's mother said.

His grandma was mad, but this was her daughter and deep down in her heart she wanted to believe her.

"Huh, take this and just get out," Hope's grandma said in dis-appointment and gave her a few bags. "I'm not giving you no money. I gotta take care of your kids, now get out."

Hope's mama took the good stuff, knowing she was making a bad decision. A bad decision yes, but she was dope sick, so she thought fuck it. She walked into the kitchen with the dope balled up in her hand and clenching onto her stomach in pain.

Hope had hurt in his eyes. He wanted to just hug his mama, but her drug habit showed no love for him, so he wouldn't allow it. He watched her with her head hung low not looking their way as she headed towards and out the door without a word.

Truth jumped up from his chair at the kitchen table and threw the playing cards across the room in anger.

"She ain't gonna stop fuckin' with that shit," he said, storming off.

"Truth!" their grandma called his name, but it did no good because he was out the front door of the house.

Truth at the age of sixteen years old had more money and women than the average adult male. He was a handsome, funny, smooth talking, and ill-tempered player who hustled from sunup to sundown. Girls from everywhere flocked to him, loving the way he dressed and smelled. Truth liked girls, but he loved money. Lots and lots of money. He wore big, flashy jewelry, which explained a little bit about what he was truly worth, and a pistol to protect himself and his wealth. Truth groomed his little brother, Hope, about the game through the pain of watching their mother withdraw from them.

Truth was blinded by anger, he was hurt and abandoned by his mother, but he had Hope. His little brother ran out the door behind him.

"Aye! Truth, aye Truth! Holdup bruh!" Hope called out as he ran towards Truth at full speed. "Aye, man, stop!" Truth was mad but he slowed up his pace so Hope could catch up with him.

"Dang! Bruh, I know you hot right now. Man, mom's gonna get better," Hope said trying to console his big brother.

"Man, Hope fuck that! She ain't shit to me, she ain't shit to us, a'ight? Why she can't even tell us she love us? Huh?" Truth was lashing out his truth. Hope walked beside him listening to the pain both of them were enduring. As they continued walking further, they ventured away from the house, not realizing how vulnerable they both were.

The streets' vocabulary ain't soft. The streets couldn't give two fucks about your personal problems. They had unauthorized movement. Truth was venting and Hope was listening but at the same time Hope was watching a tall dude behind his brother, who was walking fast while trying to be restrained by a small girl.

"Hope you hear me? She ain't shit!" Truth yelled. Hope could hear him, but he was also trying to figure out what all the commotion was about behind his brother.

"Aye, bruh, I don't—" Hope's words were cut off by Truth's anger.

"She ain't never gonna be shit to me." By the time those words left Truth's mouth he left off his feet, falling to the ground from being shoved in the back by someone.

The thirteen-year-old Hope froze in his tracks looking surprised up at the six-foot-five-inch monster standing over his brother as he laid on the ground.

"My bitch ain't shit to you?" Truth laid on the ground looking confused and reaching at his side.

"Nigga, who tha fuck is you?" Truth asked, trying to buy himself some time so he could up his pistol and pop this big nigga.

"You've been fuckin' my bitch and she ain't shit to you, huh?" Vic said, wanting to know his woman's worth.

"Vic stop, stop, leave him alone!" Gabby screamed, swinging and pounding on Vic's back with her tiny fists. Truth took that fighting chance to pull his gun but then realized it wasn't on him. This part of the dream always had Hope sweating bullets, moaning and groaning in his sleep. Hope continued to relive the internal pain that inflamed his rage. *Back in his dream, Vic had snatched Gabby off his back and pushed her away from him.*

"You takin' up for this nigga… is you crazy? You in love with him?" Vic asked, looking dismantled.

Truth jumped up from the ground.

"Playboy you comin' at me over this hoe?" he confronted Vic as Hope stood next to his brother ready to bang.

"Get back bruh, go home man," Truth told his little brother.

"Nah, I ain't going nowhere," Hope told him.

"A hoe? You calling my woman a hoe, a hoe? You callin'…you callin'," Vic was pausing and repeating his words as he lifted up his shirt and removed the chunky Glock 9-millimeter from his

waistline. Vic's eyebrows were high on his forehead and he had a crazed look on his face.

"A hoe!" Vic's head was starting to lean to the side during the rhetorical questioning.

"Hope run! Get outta here!" Truth yelled, believing his brother would honor his demand, but Hope was stubborn and didn't bulge an inch. "Hope get outta here man," Truth continued to beg his brother to leave. A crowd of people had arrived and watched the tense situation as it unfolded.

"Nigga, you gone' shoot me in front of my brother?" Truth said, stepping in front of Hope shielding him from the gun. Vic kept the Glock 9 mm aimed right at Truth's face and then looked at the boy standing behind him. He could see the fear in Truth's little brother's eyes as the kid held onto Truth. Vic wasn't a real killer; he was just heartbroken and had lost control of himself. This was totally out of his character. Vic looked around and became aware of the onlookers.

"What in the hell am I doing?" he asked himself and slowly started lowering his gun.

Once again, Gabby tried to intervene on Truth's behalf.

"You just need to stop!" she yelled, standing on the side of Vic then she continued.

"I'm not fuckin' with you no more, Vic, you need to move around. Can't you see I'm in love with him?" Gabby said, standing out in public staring down Vic and confessing her love for the outside dick which was now controlling her mind.

Right then and there, Truth looked at Hope, laying eyes on him for the last time. He knew Gabby's loving remarks for him had just ended his life. Forgiveness for his mother sat in his heart right at that moment.

Vic's legs became weak, and he couldn't stop the gun from raising back up in Truth's face.

POP! POP!

The gun went off twice. Hope felt the warm and thick wet sensation of his brother's blood and brain fragments splatter and scatter all over him while watching Truth's body drop to the ground and go into convulsions. It looked like he was humping the pavement.

"Ahhh…" Hope's helpless eyes never left his dead brother's shaking body but he could hear the screams coming from the girl running and being chased down by Vic.

POP! POP!

His little ears heard more gunshots in the distance and suddenly all the girl's screaming stopped. Then Hope began to hear a man yelling and sobbing, calling out to God. What did I do! Hope flinched after hearing another fatal gunshot, then it got silent. He no longer heard Vic calling God's name anymore.

"Ahhh…" Hope awakened from his own madness and the nightmare was over. He then realized the world was a much scarier place now that a demon was awakened. He wiped the sweat from his face, got up, and stared at himself in the mirror.

Chapter Twelve

In a matter of a few days too much had happened. Gunsmoke, empty shell casings, and dead bodies had been found on the regular. Gunshot victims kept checking in at the ER desk. It seemed to be warfare out on the streets and the aftermath wasn't pretty. Who said the streets were all fun and games? Who said when the heats on and you got flames under your ass you won't squeal like a pig, ya dig?

With one look, the police already knew he wasn't built for this.

"Cap, that's what they call you right?" Detective Myers asked him a real simple question. The detective's breath reeked of whiskey as he held a toothpick in his mouth and smelled like he had smoked three packs of squares. His hair was slicked back and pulled into a tight ponytail, and he looked as if he hadn't shaved in a couple of days, perhaps due to his heavy caseload, but at the current moment, he was locked and loaded on Cap's ass.

Cap sat up in the hospital bed forgetting all about the pain in his shoulder and head. He saw the door to his hospital room open and who came in wasn't who he expected to see. It was three more police officers. Unlike the black leather coat and blue jeans detective Myers wore, they were wearing their traditional blue uniform, trademark of the police.

"Nope, that's not Mama. Those guys are my friends, and me and my friends have been trying to talk with you for days, but your mother wouldn't let us. Good thing for us Mommy can't be around all the time. Now can she, Cap?" Detective Myers said as he moved the wooden toothpick around in his mouth using his tongue. Cap's heart started thumping so hard, he thought he might be having a heart attack but he was too young for that.

"What did I do?" Cap asked looking nervous and scared. The fear in his voice and the look on his face made the police bust out in laughter.

"Ha, ha, ha, ha, ha, whoa there, now hold on tough guy. You just let me do all the questioning here. Understand me kid?" Detective Myers told him, laying down a few ground rules, so everybody in the room knew their place.

"Cap," the detective stopped talking because he kept seeing the funny look on Cap's face every time he said his name. "What is this funny look you keep giving me when I say your name kid? Oh! Okay, okay I see what's going on. You thought I didn't know your nickname. Well listen up kid. Play time is over. Do you know where you are? Well, let me tell you. You are lying in a hospital bed with a gunshot wound to your shoulder and your head is swollen from a broken nose and a fractured skull in several places. I didn't come here to play games with you. This is serious business; you hear me, kid?" Cap nodded his head yes.

The whiskey breath seemed to grow stronger as detective Myers continued to talk. He stopped standing at the foot of Cap's hospital bed.

"You know what?" he said, as he took the toothpick from his mouth and pointed it in Cap's direction. He continued to talk to him in a calm manner. "I understand it," he explained to Cap. He eased over to the wall so he could play with the light switch. Detective Myers was dimming the lights in the hospital room to set an intimate tone and switch the mood. "Have you seen your beautiful girlfriend lately? There's nothing like your first love. That's a very special bond for a boyfriend and girlfriend Cap, and from what I hear, you love your girlfriend with all your heart. Is this true? You know what, don't answer that. Tell you what, when we're done here, you and I will take a little stroll down the hallway so you can see the girl you love with all your heart, alright?" he laughed.

Cap's scary ass once again nodded his head for a second time.

"Yes! Body language. I love it!" Detective Myers clapped his hands together once and continued to speak with great excitement. "I love it, I love it, you know what Cap, my friend?"

Detective Myers stopped and quickly covered his mouth with one hand as if he'd said something wrong. The other police in the room chuckled at the comical antics he was using.

"Wait a minute! I am sorry, is it alright if I call you my friend?" he stood extremely close to Cap, while asking permission to be his friend. The room was in total silence except for the dialogue coming from the television. Cap looked up at the intoxicated detective and then over to the three tight faced uniformed police standing at the door waiting on his response. Detective Myers raised his thin eyebrows and took notice to what had Cap's attention.

"Oh well you already know those guys are my friends but what I want to know is, can we… you…" he said, pointing his stinking toothpick right in Cap's face, "and me be friends?" Then he paused and flashed a huge drunken smile with the toothpick hanging from the corner of his mouth.

Cap started sweating like crazy and trembling under the sheets.

At his response, the detective laughed again. "Body language, I just love it. Calm down, calm down, you're sweating and shivering. It's gonna be okay. I promise you, I'm only here to be your friend, and by the way you look, you can use a friend like me. I'm not like the guy who shot you and beat you and your girlfriend up," he waved his arms in front of him and shook his head. "No, I'm totally the opposite." Then he patted his chest with one hand. "See, me, I'm an opportunist, and you and I and my friends here have an opportunity to catch the fucker who did this to you!" the detective spoke with such conviction as he pointed his finger at Cap. Cap was listening to the man's soul felt words and understood what was going on. This wasn't a trick, the police wanted him to trick on the person that had harmed him. While Cap was soaking up all the information he had received, the detective startled him.

"Wait!" he yelled pointing his finger up to the ceiling. "Before you let me know if you wanna be my friend or not, how about we all take a walk down the hall and pay a visit to your girlfriend so you guys can talk? How about that? You like that idea? I know I like that idea," he said bragging on his own thoughts. Then he staggered a little bit, going over to grab a wheelchair from in the corner of the room.

Today was one of those days. The police were everywhere on the hospital floor, and a lot of different things were going down on this wing. Two doors down the hallway from Cap's hospital room, there were a whole different set of cops standing around chitchatting and dropping donut crumbs on the floor as they waited on the patient to wake up. He was lying in the hospital bed under sedation and unaware of his current condition or new position in life. He went from predator to prey in less than a day and nine times out of ten he was going to need to pray over this.

The hardcore killer named Maytag opened his eyes to discover he had become a victim. The frown on his face showed the confusion he was hit with. Something wasn't right, he felt like something was missing in his life, but couldn't put his foot on it. He couldn't remember much but what little he could remember didn't match the environment he was seeing.

"Tha fuck goin' on?" he asked himself, coughing as he looked around still confused.

"Huh, what tha fuck they doing and where the fuck am I at?" he said, looking crazed and wondering why he was surrounded in a room crammed with police. Maytag went to move his arms but couldn't do it due to the fact the handcuffs around both his wrists kept him at bay.

"What happened, what tha fuck ya got me cuffed up fo', I ain't do shit. Let me out these muthafuckas, mane!" he yelled in the middle of the room as he was surrounded by officers. Not one time did it cross his muthafuckin' mind why he was lying in a hospital bed.

A cop wearing his badge around his neck and dressed in plain clothes approached him.

"Aye! Shut up. I got a job to do."

"You shut tha fuck up!" Maytag yelled back at him.

"Yeah, well you have the right to remain silent but you wanna talk shit. You are under arrest for murder," the plain clothes cop told him. It was only the first of many more charges filed against him.

"Murder?" he yelled out being shocked almost to death. "I ain't killed no muthafuckin' body!" he kept yelling to the police.

Maytag tried to get up but he couldn't move either one of his legs.

"Un-huh, what tha…" He looked down to see where his feet used to be.

"Aaaaahhhhh! Aaahh! My legs! My legs! Awww, nahhh! Where's my legs? Aww nah, God, nah! What happened to me, mane? Aaahh! Where's my muthafuckin' legs mane? Where'd they go?" Maytag yelled out and started weeping over his loss. He was wilding out yanking his arms in the steel cuffs. The hospital bed was moving all over the place.

"Nah, nah! Not my legs, God!" Maytag was fucked up in the head now. That's because he knew his ass was through. He would never be able to stand on shit again.

"My legs! Awww, God, nah, nah! Not my legs, mane!" he cried and cried and cried. The police stood around halfway smirking at the man lying in the bed crying his heart out and hurting bad. "My legs!" It was over for Maytag, he would never be the same, he would only be half the man he used to be.

Ke-Ke's skin had goose bumps from hearing a grown man screaming and crying in the hospital room next to hers. She was trying to lean on her brand-new, state-of-the-art crutches, but she couldn't escape the scary screaming and crying coming from next door or the police who had her held captive.

"Don't y'all need to help that man next door crying over his bad legs or something? I'm tired," she told the policeman questioning her.

"I'm sure you're tired. We are tired, but we need to go over this again, Okay? So, can you tell us what happened one more time? You said before that you got out the car and walked past the green car and saw a masked man running across the parking lot carrying a gun and that's when you heard gunshots ring out… and that's when you fell to the ground and saw you were struck by the rapid gunfire correct?" he asked her.

"Yeah, correct, correct, correct now, can I go please?" she said, running out of patience.

"I know this can be frustrating, but we need to know all the facts. Now what I would like to know is, and this is very important, right before all this happened what were you and your friend doing and what made you go to that particular gas station given its bad reputation and all?" The policeman's curiosity was prying in on Ke-Ke's privacy. She rolled her eyes and screamed at the police.

"What the fuck does it matter what I was doing before I got shot?" The policeman looked angered at Ke-Ke for not cooperating and wanting to answer his last question.

"Don't make me put you under arrest," he threatened her. She stood up with her crutches under her armpits.

"Arrest me for what? I'm the one shot here, and you talking about taking me to jail? I can't believe this. I'm the victim and y'all on some stupid shit like this!" she told the law about the injustice she was faced with.

"Look, Missy Pooh, first things first. You weren't shot, you were only grazed on the thigh by a bullet," he said downplaying Ke-Ke's injury. Then he got back on foxy business.

"Second, I can do what the fuck I want, and if you don't answer my fucking question, your little hot ass is going to jail for obstruction of justice," he told Ke-Ke, because he was tired of asking. Her mouth dropped in shock, and she had some words of her own for him.

"Uh-humm Missy Pooh, who fuckin' name is Missy Pooh? And to answer your question Sir, whatever I was doing before I got shot, muthafucka is my muthafuckin' business and on that note you need to handle ya business playa' because I ain't got shit else to say to yo bitch ass." Ke-Ke stuck her arms out as a gesture for them to put the handcuffs around her tiny wrists and take her to jail because from that moment on she was going to keep her lips sealed.

"So that's how you want to play it, Missy Pooh?" he asked. Ke-Ke kept her arms stretched out and rolled her eyes with her lips twisted. The policeman who was doing the questioning looked at his coworkers cross-eyed with impatience.

"What the hell you guys waiting for? Would somebody please cuff her up!" he gave a direct order. Ke-Ke was on her way to jail.

Meanwhile, the crying next door continued. The detective didn't want to walk over the facts and was refreshing his memory, but Maytag had no legs, and he wasn't trying to kick it. The detective kept on talking anyway.

"See while you and your friend were sitting in the car with your guns in hand contemplating on shooting the boy walking up to the gas station or probably getting ready to rob the place, little did you know, you guys were only sitting ducks getting ready to be plucked. Right now, we can't tell exactly where he came from. A masked gunmen came out of nowhere, running across the parking lot, shooting at everything and everybody. Really making it hard for us to figure out who initially was the intended target but what we do know from the gas station surveillance camera is this… forty-four shots were fired that night and the man riding in the passenger seat of your car was struck twice in the head and three times in the chest. That killed him instantaneously and made the muscles in his body lock up. Your friend died with his finger on the trigger which led to him accidentally shooting you in the car. Leaving you with the loss of your legs. Sorry to say, you lost your legs due to friendly fire," the detective informed him. Maytag's crying paused at what had been revealed. This shit couldn't be real, the killer looked dumbfounded, and his red teary eyes stared at the detective in disbelief as the detective shot back at him a smile.

"Yup, I know," the detective said, nodding his head up and down as he continued to share his thoughts with Maytag.

"I couldn't believe it either. What're the odds of that happening? Well, it's all on tape and that's what happened to you, buddy," the detective said, while patting his hand on Maytag's shoulder.

"Yup, it was your buddy. He's the one who shot your legs off. By the time we arrived bullet holes were everywhere, and you sat in your car unconscious with your gun in hand never firing off a shot and a headless body leaning on this shoulder right here," the detective said, still touching Maytag's shoulder.

"Oh, don't worry. We have pictures in the event your case goes to trial," he and the rest of the police occupying the room laughed it up. At that moment, the only thing that came to Maytag's mind was how he last remembered seeing his daughter and he hung his head low and went back to letting the tears flow. The police had him trapped in their custody and they continued to mentally fuck him up.

"You're a career criminal and I bet you know, if somebody is killed while a felony is being committed, then whoever committing the crime is charged with murder even if he didn't pull the trigger. Sucks for you. You're a convicted felon with a gun found sitting in your lap at a murder scene. Ouch!" the detective said, telling the harsh truth Maytag had to live with on top of losing his legs. Outside Maytag's hospital room the hallway had so many detectives and uniformed officers that it looked like a police precinct instead of a hospital. It was hard for the regular hospital employees to perform their job duties.

The staff could be heard murmuring, "I can't believe how many police are up here, Sam," the frustrated nurse complained using the doctor's first name. They moved carefully through the crowd and tried not to rub up against any of the officer's service pistols.

"Excuse me," the nurse said politely and flashed a trained professional smile feeling uncomfortable.

The light shined down once again; heaven helped Wiggles get out that jam. He slowly inched his way off the hospital bed so he could go take a piss in the bathroom.

"Ooo, aaah," Wiggles cried from the pain applied by unknown pressure he felt not meant for him. He took the walker next to the bed and hobbled with it in front of him to the toilet. He moved through the room on the walker and dressed in a white gown feeling like some old ass man in a nursing home.

Wiggles used the bathroom and then began to check himself out in the mirror. He lifted the gown to see three bloody bandages taped over the open wounds where the bullets grazed and ripped flesh from his left arm, shoulder, and lower leg.

"Aaaah," he said, letting the gown fall back down and was about to come out until his sensitive ears overheard a conversation between his nurse and a doctor who was entering the room.

"Sam this is really scary. Are you sure they want him, too?" she asked.

"Yes, they said him, too. The police said they will be down here to question this patient in a few minutes. I believe they said they were just waiting for a parole officer or something. So, I want you to make sure you change his bandages and I'll make sure he's coherent," the doctor laid out the game plan.

"Where is he?" the nurse asked as she was surprised the patient wasn't laying in the bed. They looked at each other confused and then their eyes scanned the congested hospital room. That's when they heard the toilet flush.

"He's up walking around already?" Shocked, the nurse looked at the doctor.

"Yeah, well I guess so," the doctor replied as he walked over and knocked on the closed bathroom door. "Are you okay in there?" he asked in a fake friendly voice as if concerned. Wiggles pushed the door so hard with force, it flung open and almost hit the doctor in his face. The nurse screamed at the loud impact of the door colliding with the wall. The rattled doctor's heart was beating fast. He and the nurse both watched Wiggles move slowly using the walker as he crept out the bathroom.

"I'm cool, fam," Wiggles coldly told the doctor and the nurse how he was feeling as he passed by hobbling on the walker and dragging the injured leg, while mean mugging both of them.

"When am I getting out of here, Doc, huh?" Wiggles asked, but he was only trying to see how things were going to play out and if he had to fuck the doctor up.

"Aww, kid don't worry about that," the doctor said winking his eye and flashing a smile. Right there and then, Wiggles knew exactly where he was going to punch the doctor.

"Don't worry, huh? Okay, cool…at least I tried, Doc," he told the doctor estimating how much strength it was going to take to sedate the doctor and the nurse. The doctor didn't understand Wiggles' statement.

"Come again? You tried? Please have a seat, you sound a little delusional. I need to check your vitals and the nurse needs to check your wounds." Wiggles knew this was just a stall tactic for the police and his parole officer to pop up. So, he decided it was time to bust his move.

"Aww, shit Doc, I'm in pain right here." Wiggles moaned as he watched the doctor and nurse rush to his aid. At the first opportunity, Wiggles cocked back and punched the rushing doctor in the winking eye, putting him right out. The nurse paused and tried to scream but she was punched in the mouth and passed out, too. Wiggles was in so much pain but getting locked up today was not an option. He kneeled down and struck them both much harder, making sure they would sleep real good. He got up and went towards the door and opened it just enough to see the police deep in the hallway a few doors down. And a few doors down was all he needed. Wiggles looked back to see the doctor and the nurse still snoring, stretched out on the floor. He slipped out the door and blended in with a large family walking past.

"Could y'all help me to my friend's room please?" he asked them with a sickly look on his face.

"Oh, sure we can, come on," the family responded and escorted him to the elevator doors and waited until he got on.

"Thank you," Wiggles said, showing his appreciation as the doors closed.

Detective Myers walked behind Cap's wheelchair and noticed a patient talking with his family standing at the elevator and felt like something wasn't right, but he had been drinking so he ignored them and continued to stay on Cap's ass. They turned the corner in the hall and stopped in front of Cap's girlfriends' hospital room.

"Alright, here we go. Let's go in so you can talk to the love of your life," he said, standing behind Cap and nodded his head for an officer to open the door. The door slowly opened, and Cap couldn't see her just yet. *Beep…beep…beep* that sound meant she was still alive but when the door fully opened he could see her clearer.

"Ahhh…is that her? That ain't her, that ain't her," Cap said with his head turned, not wanting to look at his girlfriend.

"Yeah, that's your woman lying there with that big ass head, almost about to die. Now tell me friend, who did this to her?"

Detective Myers said and grabbed Cap's head forcing him to look at her. Cap started gagging on his own vomit.

"Who did this, huh? Who did it Cap?" he yelled and then nodded at another one of the officers who walked up and punched Cap in the midsection, making him throw up what he was gagging on.

"Hope! Hope! His name is Hope!" Cap screamed at the top of his lungs with vomit dripping from his chin.

"Hope! Hope tried to kill us!" he paused to cough, "A'ight? His muthafuckin' name is Hope," Cap told the police what they wanted to know.

Detective Myers laughed. "I knew you were a little bitch and that's probably why your girlfriend is lying there looking like death. I would never have a little bitch like you for a friend. Thanks, because you just made my job much easier. Matter of fact, why don't you be a real man and spend some time with your girl," he said as he pushed the wheelchair into the beeping room and closed the door.

In the hospital basement stretched out naked, on a cold autopsy table is how the chapter ends. Finito was finished and there was nothing else to be said about him except he went out shooting his gun, so what if it was his own man he shot? Friendly fire, what the fuck is that? Ain't no such thing. What's so friendly about getting shot by a friend? Street scriptures.

Chapter Thirteen

There was no need to be friendly because from what he understood, friends could get you killed. Hope's nightmares had him thinking about Truth, his dead brother. He didn't give a fuck about nothing. Hope felt it was time for him to turn up. Before Truth was murdered in cold blood over a bitch, he had just bought himself a car. Truth's paper was long and no expense was spared when he bought the car. It was an electric blue, racing performance, 1984 Cutlass Oldsmobile with custom painted white leather interior and the Billet steering wheel. It also had a shift kit in the wood grain console between the bucket seats. The Billet rims and letter tires made the Cutlass Oldsmobile a trophy winner.

In tribute to his brother, Hope pulled the car out the garage with the engine running like brand new. Covered in a white hoodie and in his lap laid the FN-Five-SeveN fully loaded, Hope's foot hit the gas pedal and the Billet rims and letter tires spung around in place. He fishtailed out his grandma's driveway and turned up the music. The underground sound of the rapper Chaos Da Don's song "Aggravated Murda" was pounding so hard through the two fifteen-inch JL audio speakers that it sounded like the trunk was going to bust the fuck open. The super-fast lyrical word play and slow beat with a deep bass put a mean mug on Hope's face. Chaos Da Don was spitting that shit he was on.

"*Close your eyes and visualize, internal cries from a thug nigga, on a journey to the grave it's a young street slave, with a Glock, pushing rocks on the block getting paid, for the shit that I crave these days, bitch be gassing me, like I care, if they mad at thee, fuck yo chief, and majesty. A renegade in the land, in the flesh, I'm a tragedy. Bow down, while I read you the law. Break bread with the click, talk slick here the barrel cough niggaz wannabe plugged, you shall shock from a slug. No love, ya life last, from a sawed off. Gotcha laying on your back, and ya pulse start to crawl, and ya tears start to fall. A sudden death, no doubt caught slippin', in the quest of my murderous route eternally, the dark spirit, that you heard about a fallen angel, born in a world of sin. I do the dirt that hurt, the deepest part in the heart of men, the book of Revelations, is my friend the prophecies at the end, to send you back to your maker again. So, pray to God that we never meet, 'cause yo' time is up. To catch my wrath, in the midst of the street love agony, so prepare for defeat 'cuz the flame I spit, got the devil trying to run from my heat. These muthafuckuz wanna think I'm a lame like it's a game they change, you want drama-want to challenge my name I'm too thorough, when I'm bringing the pain. I tear you straight from the frame, a real nigga gon' re-main the same, I keep it burnin', like it's acid rain- going straight for ya brain from the start. Plan to tear you apart sealing your fate 'cuz you can't relate. A warrior striking fear in your heart.*

"It wuz a murda, 'cuz I'm like the reaper and made a nigga, see the flatline aggravated murda, destroying all competition and niggaz thinking, they can take mine, it was a murda, 'cuz I murda my foes and left a nigga full of bullet holes 'cuz they thought it was sweet, I pack heat puttin' niggaz to sleep. My eyes red, from the weed I chief."

It was a bright sunshiny day in the midst of winter. The crazy part about it was the frozen white snow made it look even brighter outside. Riding through the streets switching lanes punching the gas, he was moving too fast, Hope had accumulated a few bodies and his name was now being mentioned in connection to the recent violence in the past day or so. Although the murders involving him were still a mystery to the streets and to the police, what he didn't know was what lay ahead was going to hurt him. While he was breezing through traffic, Cap's bitchass had been in the hospital boo'hooing and name dropping. Hope was turning up on niggas and niggas had the police about to turn up on his Black ass.

The Cutlass was rolling and had letter tires running past other cars and traffic like a race car on the speed track. The music was pounding, and Hope's cold heartless eyes watched the streets and thoughts of his deceased brother entered his mind. His face frown up in anger. Hope grabbed the steering wheel with both hands and drove a little faster in the car and in life. Then the feeling the hurt of losing his mother made him slow down a bit. He remembered how his mother looked lying in the casket. His past made him start to feel like he was a soldier of misfortune. The traffic lights up ahead had turned red and with the white hoodie over his head, Hope played with death. He blew right through the busy four-way intersection flexing. He was now a hazard for whoever was making plans to get in his way, he knew they were going to meet a disastrous end. Shit was real, Hope only had three things for a nigga and that was murder, death, and to kill.

He shot past the car wash on State Street.

"Fuck it," he said, making a quick decision to get the Cutlass washed. Hope slowed down then whipped the steering wheel like a pro and busted a U-turn in the middle of the street. Hope smashed on the gas and flew back down the street until he turned into the already packed car wash's parking lot. Hope saw a worker he knew standing there looking cold as hell and pulled up on him. Hope rolled the driver's side window down first then he preceded to turn the music down so he could talk.

"Aye, yo! Tiger what's up?" Hope called out the dude's name from his warm car.

The dude named Tiger had scars across his face and stood there putting money in the side pocket of a black coat embroidered with Mirror Affect written on the back, representing the car wash's service logo. Hope watched him stroll over to the car. Tiger was one of the niggas that came from what was known as the Old Testament of Street Scriptures. Hope remembered riding out to the projects with his big brother as a shorty and seeing Tiger out there wild and crazy acting with the biggest bottle of Seagram's gin the liquor store could sell legally and each time Tiger saw him, he was in the car with Truth. He would reach in his pocket and pull out one of the biggest knots of money. Hope remembered seeing him too, and Tiger would bless him with twenty dollars just on the strength he was Truth's little brother. Then Truth and Tiger would disappear behind one of the project buildings. Each visit they would never walk behind the same building twice as it was always different every trip.

Hope was sitting in the car and watched all the folks standing out there gambling and drinking, smoking blunts and hustling with their guns out in the open, running up to cars making fast cash. A few minutes went by and Truth would pop back up out of nowhere and hop back in the car. Before pulling off he would always make sure the large chunks of white stuff wrapped and tied up in a light tan plastic grocery bag was secured on him. Then he would tell Hope to put his seat belt on, so the police wouldn't have any particular reason to pull him over on his way to the crib.

Tiger had learned his life lessons through prison bars and street inflicted scars and felt a need to change before a seventeenth District Judge in the county of Winnebago gave him a sentence with numbers that didn't come with change or even worse becoming change over something that didn't make sense. Tiger made a conscious decision which left him where he was and that was not standing outside in the projects but outside in the cold washing cars before going back behind bars. He walked up to the car and gave Hope a handshake with his cold hand.

"What's good lil' pimping? I see you brought the Truth out," Tiger said, referring to Hope's brother's car. Tiger looked around still stuck in his street mentality, he was making sure his surroundings was cool and then he went back to popping corn with Hope.

"This muthafucka still looks good. Whatcha tryin' to do, you trying to get washed up?" Tiger said peeping the gun in Hope's lap and understood his reasons for keeping it on him.

"Yeah Tiger, can you get me in and out?" he asked him. Tiger looked at all the cars in the parking lot.

"Yeah, I gotcha, pull in the back and I'ma let you in the garage, a'ight?" he said, showing love for Hope. Hope drove the car back to where the garage door was and heard other cars honking their horns on some hatin' shit.

"Shut the fuck up," Hope mumbled and turned his music back up. The bass booming and the trunk was sending vibrations through the ground and into the other cars parked out there pissing people off even more. If anybody has something to say, they would be doing so at their own risk.

Hope parked the car and hopped out. He left the FN-Five-SeveN on the driver's seat but that didn't mean he was without a gun on him. He stood back with the hoodie over his head looking at people sitting in their cars as they complained and watched him. A few faces sitting in the cars looked familiar to him from the card game the other night where he had to perform. Hope took his hands and pulled the hoodie from over his head so he could reveal who he was. He watched the people that were there as they saw him in action. They quickly shut their mouths, dropped their heads and looked away praying and asking God why he hadn't warned them that was him.

Hope went back to minding his own business in a now quiet environment where he could hear his music playing without the interruption of car horns. Tiger was washing the car and bringing it back to life. The sun was shining down on his work and the car had a sharp glare coming from it. Then he cleaned the rims to perfection and sprayed the letter tires with something he called *Wet-Wet* and then he wiped the white letters on the tires, so they were clean and looked extra white like when he was in the streets, Tiger took what he did seriously. Even though he was washing cars he tried to be the best at it. Hope stood outside watching the streets and Tiger finished up on the car wiping it down.

"Alright Hope, you back down," Tiger told him. Wishing he could tell him more than that but the facts were what they were and everybody had to find out on their own what the streets had to offer.

"Okay, cool. Huh, here you go Tiger," Hope said and gave him the money for the car wash. Hope pulled this hoodie back over his head and got into the spotless cleaned car. Hope was about to close the car door, but he had a question for Tiger that wouldn't let him leave yet. Tiger was counting a much smaller bankroll and was looking at how many more cars he had to wash in order to make ends meet.

"Aye, Tiger what made you quit the game and stop drinking?" Hope had to ask him before he smashed out. Tiger paused from counting the chump change in his hands, but he never looked at Hope.

"I found out through experience. It's either you quit the game and live or play the game until the end or it kills you. The game plays you, you don't play the game. And I stopped drinking because I wasn't thirsty to die anymore. Feel me?" he said giving Hope his reasons as he went back to counting his money. Hope looked at the crazy nigga he used to know and closed the car door. He stared at Tiger for a moment who was still counting his money. Then he put the gun back in his lap.

"Different strokes for different folks," Hope said and honked his horn to Tiger out of respect and peeled off with the music blasting and mugging the other people in the car wash parking lot.

Hope turned on the street and shot off like a bat out of hell.

"It wuz a murda, cuz I'm like the reaper and make a nigga see the flatline aggravated murda, destroying all competition and niggaz thinkin' they can take my mind, it was a murda cuz I murda my foes and left a nigga full of bullet holes cuz they thought it was sweet, I pack heat, putting niggaz to sleep. My eyes red, from the weed I chief."

Chapter Fourteen

Who said farmers out in the cornfields weren't smart? A brief history lesson about the city of Rockford Illinois. Originally Rockford was labeled as a town, it went from having one courthouse and maybe five jail cells to what it is today. It was said to get certified the officials conspired in barns to become a city and crime was going to be the cornerstone of that endeavor. Much like today, trumped up charges and bogus convictions commissioned the foundation for the city. Drugs, bullets, and blood is what led to the building of one federal courthouse building. The old jail facility, which was called the Rockford Public Safety Building, was closed in 2007 but was still utilized for court appearances and hearings.

In the heart of the crooked city, police pulled bloody criminals through the doors of the new jail system which is now called the Winnebago County Justice Center. The new facility was known for pushing criminals out on high ass bonds. Out of fear, they created and spread three satellite holding police precincts through-out the city in specific areas of town. One was built right outside of the Rockford Housing Projects as a divine sign, it was devised to keep order for them niggas on that space age government plan-tation. The police rode around letting folks know to be cool, oth-erwise they'd be locked down twenty-three and one, and made to order commissary once a week for up to five years. And as for the shorties out in the streets who were running wild, there was a ju-venile courthouse building waiting to sentence them to do time on the outskirts of the city limits in a brand-new detention center that had been built just for them. The facility was located by the bridge near the new toll booths on the far north-side of town. In a small city of 149,000 people, the numbers didn't seem to add up for a nigga. Four county courthouses and five jail houses with twenty-three and one, the odds ain't in a nigga's favor. Anyone who had experienced that life knew coming out of jail for one hour in the county was hell.

It took one shot of whiskey and less than one hour to find Hope in the database of the Rockford police department's com-puter system. Hope's picture came across the computer screen.

"Wow, are you fucking kidding me? He looks like a baby, there's no way this face did that to those people," Detective Myers said, surprised by what he had discovered while looking at the ju-venile mugshots. It threw him off so much that he needed to take another shot of whiskey real quick.

The mutilating damage couldn't have been caused by the kid he saw on the mug shot. Detective Myers went back through the database to see if he could find somebody else who might've coincidentally had the same name as Hope, but this time with a different picture that matched the fucked-up shit he had witnessed at the hospital. The detective thought it was worth a shot, but he came up short. There was not another person in the system with the name Hope, there was only the cute kid he saw on the screen. So, Detective Myers stood up and walked back and forth in front of the computer screen still amazed.

At that moment, another detective walked up and saw Hope's mug shot on the computer screen.

"Myers how's it going? You look troubled about something," that detective said as he peered over his shoulder to check on him. Detective Myers took a toothpick out of his mouth and pointed at the mug shot on the computer screen.

"I'm working a case and this shit's not making any fucking sense. There is no way this kid right here did what I saw at the hospital. This face could never have put the fear of God in the guy I questioned earlier today. His name is Hope, with a name like Hope this kid couldn't possibly be responsible for the evil lashed out on those two kids in the hospital. It just can't be," the detective said as he explained his state of confusion.

"Yeah, his name is Hope but that cute kid on that mug shot has seen more fucked up things than you can imagine. At the age of thirteen his brother's brains was shot out all over him. Then on top of that on the same day, two more people were killed right in front of him. But that's not all, a few weeks later the kid comes home and finds his mother bent up backwards on the floor dead with a needle still sticking out her arm. Then you would think his grandmother would've stopped selling heroin because of all that trauma." The detective was trying to shed some light on the situation, but detective Myers had a question of his own.

"Who is his grandmother?" Detective Myers asked. The detective looked at him like he was an alien or something of that nature.

"Who is his gramma seriously, you didn't just ask me that?" the detective asked, looking like his mind was blown by detective Myers' response.

"Come, walk with me, Myers. This will only take a minute, alright? I think maybe you need to stop drinking so much because you are way out of the loop," he told Myers and they went for a short walk.

They came to a stop as Detective Meyer saw a team of drug force task agents working in a congested room with pictures of suspects taped on a bulletin board and at the very top there was a picture of a little old lady with whitish-gray hair. He watched the agents move around in fast-paced momentum while answering two and three ringing telephones at a time. The detective pointed his finger at the top of the bulletin board.

"That's his grandma," he pointed out to Detective Myers.

Detective Myers evaluated all the pictures on the board and saw some serious hardened criminals hanging up on that wall. How could she be at the top of the pack? He knew for sure there were a few well-known killers and a couple of gang members pictures up there because he knew them personally. But and still how was this frail old lady at the top of the pack? His thoughts were interrupted when he heard one of the agents yell out over everybody in the room.

"The judge granted us a search warrant!"

Chapter Fifteen

"Boop-bop, baby, yeah-yeah," Old School was singing his own made-up tune walking down the street. In his mind, his day had been going just fine and dandy, shit couldn't be any better. He had just busted a move, cashed a fake check, and had himself a couple hundred dollars to the good. Although he didn't drink, Old School was celebrating with a high half pint of Wild Irish Rose red wine.

"Yeah, yeah, baby boop-bop." It might have been bright outside, but Old School made sure he walked in all the shady areas. He knew it was best that way, anyway he didn't need to be walking out on front street. Somebody could've been looking for him because of the bullshit he had just pulled. Old School took a sip of the harsh cheap wine.

"Ah yeah, yeah, mmm-hmm. That's it. The good stuff baby," he sang and did a little dance after his small drink. He saw the lion's den was full. Junkies and crackheads lamped around the barrel of fire still arguing and trying to beat each other out. He kept walking past the lion's den, because right now wasn't the time for that. It was time for him to get right, and he needed the nuke bomb. Old School knew exactly where to go for his forbidden pleasure. He tried to hang around on the corner in anticipation of catching his little mans' Hope slide through. He looked back and saw a fresh new chick walking with a sucker going to the lion's den.

"Awe, nah. I need some top and bottom from her," Old School said and went up to the door of Hope's grandma's house. He looked around and made sure shit was straight before he knocked on the door. Old School knocked three times on the door, the player he was. TAP! TAP! TAP! He fidgeted on the steps still looking around.

Finally, he heard a small voice ask, "Who is it?"

"It's Old School," he answered. Old School heard the locks on the door become undone and the door eased opened. He saw the little old lady hiding halfway behind the door.

"Come in," she told him, as she looked over his shoulder to see if anybody was behind him. Once he entered her lovely home, Old School saw family portraits all over the place but a crazy thing entered his mind. He noticed that most of the people in the pictures were dead or locked up in the system for life.

"Okay hurry up. What do you want?" she asked him to place his order. While he was looking at the family history on pictures,

Old School also saw the chrome pistol in her hand, so he quickly decided he'd better stop looking at pictures before his own picture was put on a T-shirt with *rest in peace* airbrushed on it.

"Huh, hit me light, like a woodpecker with a headache," Old School said, talking slick.

She looked upside his head. "Boy, you ain't told me shit, now what do you want and I ain't gonna ask you again," she said, waving the pistol in his face with her finger on the trigger. Old School had pressed in his luck and he knew he had better straighten up immediately.

"Ten, let me get ten. I apologize," he begged her pardon, pulled out a hundred-dollar bill and gave it to her.

"Okay, now that's more like it. I know you know better than to come in here playing, baby," she put the money in her pocket and pulled out a zip lock bag with about two thousand dime bags of heroin in it. She held the zip lock bag in the same hand as the gun, pointing the barrel in his direction for her safety.

"You hear that?" Old School asked her. Hope's grandma was contemplating shooting him right then and there because he was playing in her house entirely too much, and she didn't know what kind of shit his slick talking ass was up to. She continued to silently count out his ten bags so he could go on about his business.

"Huh, you don't hear that?" he asked her again. She looked at him like he really wanted to get shot. Then it happened.

"Police!" They both knew there was no chance to escape. The battering ram came crashing through the locked door and the door flew off the hinges like a leaf in the wind. Hope's grandma pulled the trigger, *POP! POP! POP! POP!* She sent shots at the doorway as she threw the zip lock bag of heroin in the air and tried to make a break for the back door. The first person from the S.W.A.T. team took all four hot slugs in his bullet proof vest which covered up his chest. He fell to the floor and Old School did too because the police were returning gunfire. Bullets went through furniture, knocked pictures off the walls and debris flew everywhere. Old School could hear the bullets' impact. He laid on the floor covering up his head with his arms like that was going to stop a bullet from knocking his shit back.

Then the shooting stopped and the S.W.A.T. team stormed in. Old School didn't stand a chance for what was about to happen to him.

"Aaah-aah-aah!" they were in there whooping his ass military style. They were striking him with blows and slamming his ass all over the place like a rag doll. Old School fell backwards to the floor wondering *when will it ever end?* But the S.W.A.T. team threw him in front of the door and started marching and stepping on his ass like he was a doormat.

"Aaah-aah-aah!" Old School screamed out in pain from feeling the bottom soles of the S.W.A.T. team's boots. He stopped moving and just let it happen. He was starting to see flashes of white light with each footprint coming across his face.

"All right that's enough. Cuff him up and make sure he doesn't have any weapons on him." Old School heard what sounded like the voice of God but was only the S.W.A.T. team leader giving a direct order. They were putting him in handcuffs and Old School could hear them ransacking the crib in a backroom somewhere in the house. He could hear them through the walls, it sounded like they were putting the bats on Hope's grandma's ass. They were yelling and cursing, and he could hear her little voice screaming out in pain just like he was.

They snatched him up and walked him outside. Old School's right eye was swollen, and his mouth and nose were leaking bad. The neighbors in the community came outside to see everything happening. Some of them had their phones out recording the event.

Old school could see he was in the spotlight and every junkie and crackhead was in attendance from the lion's den, even the new chick he wanted the top and bottom from. He was standing out there with his ass whooped in the custody of the police feeling embarrassed as hell. People were standing around talking about him and pointing their fingers in his direction. The police had him posted up like a billboard sign of what it looked like to get nabbed.

"Man, it's cold out here! Put me in the back of the muthafuckin' car!" Old School was ready to take his ride and was letting them know it. He could see people were still pointing at him and recording shit with their phones. And to make shit worse, he saw the new chick walk off with one of the junkies from the lion's den.

The junkie's arm was wrapped around her tiny waist as he kissed the cheek on her pretty face. Then they walked off into the sunset to have some real nasty sex. The sight made Old School sick to his stomach. Then the police started bringing devastating evidence out of the house which was going to bury somebody under two penitentiary areas: State and Feds.

"He set me up!" Hope's grandma's voice was getting louder. That's because four S.W.A.T. officers carried her out of the house by her arms and legs. They had her hog-tied and on display. Her whitish-gray hair was blood drenched and her little frail body was trying to jerk out of their grasp. The muscle-bound S.W.A.T. officers were really struggling to carry her to the truck. The first person she saw and recognized was Old School standing outside with the police.

"You, you, set me up! You told on me nigga! He's gonna kill you bitch!" she yelled at Old School with blood flying out of her mouth as though she was trying to spit on him. When she saw all the onlookers standing outside she decided to let the world know who did this to her.

"Old School set me up! Y'all hear me! Old School set me up! Y'all tell my baby Old School set me up!" she repeated the chant over and over until she was cut off by one of the guys hands covering her bloody mouth, muffling her fortune-telling. Hope's grandma was rough to handle and her mouth broke free from the S.W.A.T. guy's large hand.

"I'ma die in jail. Yeah, my baby is killing you, Old School!" she told him and was about to say more but couldn't because the S.W.A.T. guy had hit her bloody head up against the truck as he threw her in the back seat of the vehicle which resulted in her landing on her stomach. The black S.W.A.T. truck sped off down the street with her in it, leaving Old School standing in handcuffs watching everybody out there who heard what she said about him giving him a cold stare. Although he knew every word she said was false, the truth was, her words were going to get him lost in the sauce period. To discredit him even more, the S.W.A.T. team leader walked over, unlocked the handcuffs and took them off.

"Old School this is it. Get out of here before we arrest you for loitering or something. Now go on and get!" the team leader said, just signing Old School's death certificate.

Old School looked at him with tears in his eyes. As he walked away, he heard the bystanders speaking bad on his name. The game as he knew it was a done deal for him. His little life, for however long, would never be the same again. There was no doubt in his mind, Hope would be on his ass about this situation no matter what the truth was. Old School had to set shit straight or do some other shit like get Hope hit. Either way, he had to do something before Hope came after him. Decisions, decisions, Old School had some real decisions to make.

Chapter Sixteen

Wiggles knew had he not been eavesdropping, the police would've gotten the drop on him. A dirty drop wasn't going to be the reason for his incarceration. They were going to have to upgrade his charges. Wiggles decided dropping the doctor and nurse for playing those games with him so he could slip out from under the police's nose was the easy part. But he was still feeling a slight touch of dizziness, what wasn't easy was almost dying. And Wiggles knew there was no kicks and giggles in damn near coming close to ending up with his picture on a faded rest in peace T-shirt. He came only a few shots away from becoming earthbound.

Wiggles thought about how fucking around with Ke-Ke, he was almost a down to earth nigga fo' real.

"Dumb bitch," he mumbled at the thought while he waited for his cousin to come back from bonding Ke-Ke out of jail. And he couldn't wait for his cousin to bring her to him. If it wasn't for her thirsty ass acting stupid, neither of them would have been in the fucked-up situation they were in. That's how it be though, a bitch could get a nigga caught up in a jam not even trying to. Wiggles knew Ke-Ke wasn't trying to get them killed. Even though the bullets flying at the gas station was meant for them niggas in the two-tone Old green school car, he was mad at her for this shit.

In the short time he'd been fucking with her, he had been shot more than once and had a new case, plus on top of all that, he was on the run but had made it to his cousin's house. The paramedics had cut his bloody and holey clothes off him to try to save his life, so he sent his cousin out to get a brand-new outfit. Wiggles got dressed so he could look fresh. He covered the blood seeping bandages with new gauze then he put on a purple velour designer jogging suit with his gold jewels gleaming in the light to make him look just right. He finished up his look with laced up purple shoe-strings in his purple boots.

Wiggles counted the rest of the money he had from the card game and put the bundle of cash in his pocket. He could hear the loud music coming from the trunk of somebody's car parked outside on the block. In his position, the last thing he needed was undo heat. He walked to the window and peeked out.

"Man! Fuck! What's this nigga doing?" Wiggles complained at what he saw outside the window. *Again,* he thought, undo heat was something he didn't need but what he also didn't need was that nigga Hope sitting right outside his cousin's house in the car making a serve. Wiggles decided to stay put and watch the transaction take place.

"Man, this nigga needs to move the fuck around," Wiggles said, as he lit a blunt to calm his nerves, coughing. "Shit! Damn, this shit is smoking the right way," he said aloud as he complemented the good grade of weed he was blowing in the air, but he grew more frustrated as he continued to watch the illegal activity that was going down right in front of his cousin's joint.

"Come on, come on, come on, get the fuck on." Wiggles, from his safe place, was encouraging Hope to move on. The pictures hanging on the wall were shaking from the loud music coming out of the car outside. Wiggles puffed and puffed on the blunt. Smoke was released from his lungs as his eyes focused, the passenger door opened.

"'Bout muthafuckin' time," he said watching the dope fiend exit Hope's car. "Okay, Okay, cool." Wiggles continued to smoke and wait on the car to pull off but that didn't happen yet. Wiggles watched as Hope stayed parked outside even after the sale was final. Wiggles wasn't no dummy. He knew Hope must have been waiting on another customer. And just like that, as he thought, another person walked up to Hope's car. But this time instead of the individual getting in the car, Hope rolled down the window and made the fade.

"Tryna' get that money back you lost, huh?" Wiggles commented on what he was seeing and hit the blunt once more. That's when he saw the headlights of his cousin's car turn into the driveway while simultaneously, he witnessed Hope pulling off fast down the street past the roaming dope fiend.

"Yeah cuz, bring her ass here," he said as he watched as the headlights went out and the car doors opened. Wiggles moved away from the window and stood in perfect position for when the door opened. Like back at the hospital, he was on guard, and he could hear them talking outside, when they entered, he was ready. He heard the key when it entered the lock and watched the doorknob turn. The door slowly swung open.

"You first," said Wiggles' cousin to Ke-Ke being polite. She was moving on the crutches, limping her temporarily crippled self through the doorway smiling back at Wiggles' well-mannered cousin. Ke-Ke was caught by surprise as she felt a sharp sting across the side of her face. At that moment, all she could see was a white light.

"Goofy bitch!" Although her vision was gone, Ke-Ke recognized the voice responsible for the extra pain she was feeling as the crutches and she fell to the floor.

"Yo' dumbass almost got us killed! Playin' them dumb ass games!" Wiggles said watching Ke-Ke who was trying to figure out what was happening.

"Bitch, next time I tell your dumb ass to *get me out* of somewhere, get me tha' fuck out of there," he continued to let her know the real business. Once she gathered her sight, Ke-Ke could see clearly what he was saying. Her face was numb from being slapped down to the floor. From the floor she saw Wiggles dressed in purple pointing his finger at her. Meanwhile his well-mannered cousin went to pick up her crutches.

"Wiggles, I didn't know that shit was gonna happen nigga!" Ke-Ke snapped back. She wasn't trying to hear that bullshit Wiggles was talking about. They'd both gotten caught up in the crossfire and she wasn't about to take the blame for some shit that happens every single day. Who the fuck did he think he was?

"Damn! Boy, you better help me off this floor Wiggles!" she commanded him. Wiggles looked over at his cousin who was holding her crutches as if he was confused.

"What is you looking at him fo'?"

"Come, pick me up nigga!" she yelled. Wiggles' cousin laughed.

"You put her down there, pick her ass up muthafucka," he told Wiggles agreeing with Ke-Ke. Wiggles took a deep breath.

"Y'all think this is a game huh?" Wiggles said shaking his head in disappointment as he walked over to help Ke-Ke off the floor.

"You just better remember what I said," he told Ke-Ke as he was helping her up leaving a space wide open for destruction. He was looking Ke-Ke in her eyes and was wondering why in the fuck she was smiling at him. She winked her left eye at Wiggles and then gave him a four-piece spicy combo hand hook. The impact from the close-up punches hit so hard like a thunderbolt, lighting his ass up and caused Wiggles' head to jerk back and forth upon contact. He was caught off guard and involuntarily let Ke-Ke go so fast without even realizing it.

"Ahhh, bitch!" he yelled being caught in a vulnerable predicament. Ke-Ke looked like she was about to scream.

"Nah, bitch don't scream now, you think it's ah game!" she yelled back at him from down on the floor once again. Wiggles had stumbled back and fell over a chair that sat at the dining room table.

"Nigga, you betta keep your muthafuckin' hands off me!" Ke-Ke continued to let him know what it was and what it ain't gonna be in their new rocky relationship. This time she didn't need no help getting off the floor, she got up on her own accord and snatched her crutches away from Wiggles' now laughing cousin.

"Ya'll two crazy than a muthafucka'. Yeah, y'all go good together," he said giving their relationship his approval. His cousin may have been laughing and thought it was hilarious for him to be getting pieced out by Ke-Ke, but he felt much, much different when he saw what was about to happen next.

Wiggles was about to make somebody say *hallelujah in the church over Ke-Ke* because he was finna pop her ass. Suddenly, Wiggles jumped up from the floor, kicked the fallen chair across the room and pulled out a chunky .10 millimeter.

"Da fuck wrong wit' you bitch? You tryin' real hard to get killed, ain't you?" Wiggles said staring down at her. His cousin instantly ran in front of him, putting his own life on the line for Ke-Ke.

"Nah, cuz you better not shoot this bitch in my crib. Fuck wrong with you mane?" Wiggles was mad as hell and Ke-Ke was too. But she could see him Wiggles face that playtime was over.

"Cuz, I'm tellin' her some real shit and she gonna punch *me* my nigga?" Wiggles said as he cocked the gun.

"Goddamnit! Wiggles! Don't do it!" his cousin was begging him not to go back to prison. Out the corner of his eye, he could see Ke-Ke had started slowly backpedaling on her crutches.

"She done got me popped already, now she on some gangster shit hitting on me and thangs. Nah, cuz watch out for a minute," Wiggles said, pushing his cousin out the way and Ke-Ke tried to take off running. The crutches fell to the floor but not her. Wiggles grabbed her by the back of her shirt and put the gun to the back of her head.

"Bitch, you finna be sucking dick through two holes in your head," he told her and pulled the trigger. *POW!* The gun blast rung out and Ke-Ke fell to the floor.

"Wiggles! What the fuck cuz!" Ke-Ke was laying on the floor not moving a muscle. Wiggles looked over at his cousin who was holding onto his arm. They both looked down at Ke-Ke looking up at them.

"Give me this muthafuckin' gun mane until you cool off. See, that's the kind of shit I be talking about. You about to kill the bitch, and she like you. Quit being stupid and pick her ass up and take her in the room muthafucka' before you give her a reason to leave," he said and yanked the gun out of Wiggle's hand.

"Tha fuck you bond her out of jail fo?" he added. Ke-Ke's eyes were still focused on the smoke coming out the large gun barrel that was still pointed somewhat in her direction. She watched them going back and forth as her heart was pumping what seemed like a million miles a second.

Wiggles went and grabbed her by the arm.

"C'mon." Ke-Ke let him grab her up without any trouble. All she wanted to do was give him her full cooperation from here on out. He lifted her up to where she could stand on her own.

"Stay right here," he told her. Then he went and picked up the crutches. The whole time Ke-Ke was still in shock, she looked at the bullet hole in the wall and then over at Wiggles kneeling to pick up one of her crutches and then she looked over at Wiggle's cousin. He winked his eye at her as he held the gun in his hand.

"Aye, lil' cousin, I'ma leave you and your girlfriend alone so y'all can straighten things out. I'll be back later. I got some other shit to go handle. And please will y'all behave? I don't want my house fucked all up when I get back," he said and tucked the gun on his waist and pulled his shirt over it.

"Yeah cuz, we cool ain't nobody finna break shit in your house man," Wiggles told him and gave Ke-Ke her crutches.

"A'ight, cool. I'm out," Wiggle's cousin said, and headed for the door. "Oh yeah, nice meeting you again Ke-Ke. I guess I'll be seeing more of you huh?" he said and laughed his way out the door until it closed behind him.

Chapter Seventeen

ope had heard through the grapevine the news about his grandma. One of the local drunks that was staggering and feeling fine had been out in front of a liquor store as Hope approached. The drunk stopped Hope under some penny-pinching act hoping to purchase another bottle of cheap wine.

"Th-th-the police was um, um, whoopin' her ass, they ain't have to do ya grandma like dat'. I-I mean damn…iit-it hurt my heart to see them beat her like, like dat'. Hope? Ya hear me?" the drunk said with wine breath. Then he put the glass bottle that he had hiding in a wrinkled up brown paper bag up to his ashy lips and took a swig in honor of Hope's grandma's pain and then began to talk again.

"She was screamin' and hollerin' out *that nigga Old School—*"

Hope cut him off. "Old School what?"

The drunk took a quick nip at the wine bottle and then lit a cigarette and blew out the smoke. His bloodshot eyes looked at Hope and saw he was boiling over with anger.

"She said that nigga set her up," the drunk said nodding his head, trying to hold onto his balance and take another puff off the square at the same time. Hope became distracted and couldn't hear another word. It was like he'd went deaf and blind. The pace of his heart raced and he felt like he was losing his breath from the cold air like the cigarette the drunk was smoking. It seemed as if air was coming up short.

"Hope! Hope!" The drunk could see this wasn't good at all because the kid was no longer listening to him. Even though the drunk was under the strong influence of alcohol, his street sense acknowledged to him death was on the way.

"Fuck this shit. Let me get up out of here. Uh, Hope—" he didn't even finish his sentence. The drunk didn't want his last words to Hope to be his death sentence. So the drunk left Hope to ponder alone as he wandered off down the street.

Hope was still in a state of shock as he took out his phone to validate the drunk's story. The first thing he did was dial his grandma's phone number. His eyes watched the world with a sharpness as he held the phone to his ear. The phone just rang and rang until, "Hello? Grandma…" Hope spoke into the phone with excitement. But that was quickly derailed when the sound of an unfamiliar voice replied instead.

"Nope, sorry kiddo. You called the right number but got the wrong person." Hope's heart dropped and almost stopped.

"Who dis'?" he asked already knowing the answer.

"Good question…but let me do the questioning. Where are you sport? We have an arrest warrant for you." Hope removed the phone from his ear and looked at it crazy. Then he put it back to his ear.

"You tweakin', tha' fuck I look like, I don't talk to the police but I'ma tell you this…I heard what y'all did to my grandma." Hope hung the phone up before the police could make a rebuttal. He jumped in his car and slowly pulled out the liquor store's parking lot with a lot on his mind.

He and time was lost, Hope drove around with nowhere to go. The gas in the car was getting low. He pulled up at another gas station and pulled the white hoodie over his head. Hope hopped out the car and paid for the gas.

"Yo, aye, aye, pump my gas!" he yelled to a pan handler as he was standing around and gave him a dollar for the duty and then he got back in his car. Instantly, Hope received a text message from his grandma's phone.

Take a look, kiddo, it read and then a video was sent to his phone. Hope sat in the car and paused for a moment.

"What they on?" he questioned himself. Then the graphic image of his small grandmother hog tied, bloody, and being carried out of their house played over the phone's screen in his hand. The first tear fell from his eyes.

"That motherfucka' set me up!" Hope's grandma's voice was yelling through the speaker of his phone.

The clean Cutlass Oldsmobile parked at the gas pump in the parking lot of the hot, bullet hole infested gas station had Hope sitting under the bright lights at night with his world seeming so dark. Hope's heart had been snatched out his chest by the police. The helpless cries coming through his cell phone as he watched the video had him shivering. His stomach was churning, and his skin was burning. The fear and anger he was feeling was only in it's infancy. The pain going through his veins was going to make it rain bullets. His infernal temper was about to explode on the whole city. The people walking past his car going into the gas station were totally unaware of what he was about to unleash. Still looking at the footage, he could hear her voice. Hope's eyes were glued to the sensitive detail of his grandma's beautiful whitish-gray hair being disrespected with lots and lots of blood from the police busting her little head wide open to the white meat. He just sat there and cried slightly in silence.

"You, you, set me up! You told on me nigga. He's going to kill you, bitch!" Hope listened and watched her yelling at Old School as the police carried her past him. He dropped his head.

"Muthafuckin' Old School," he said gritting his teeth with his jaws tight. Right then and there at that very moment, Hope had made-up his mind, Old School's telling ass was a done deal. As soon as he saw him, Old School was getting killed and there was nothing to talk about. POW! Right in the head, knocking his brains out. It was going to be a senseless killing. Hope continued to let the tears fall where they may as he listened to his grandma tell the world the real business about who brought forth her demise.

"Old School set me up! Y'all hear me, goddamnit, Old School set me up! Y'all hear me, tell my baby, it was Old School!" ope watched the S.W.A.T. guy cover up her mouth then Hope saw the true strength in his grandma as she jerked and wrestled her mouth free until she could let her voice be heard one last time in the free world.

"I'ma die in jail! Old School," that's when the police rammed her bloody head straight into their patrol truck to do the trick of shutting her up and knocking her out cold in the same process. Hope's whole body cringed at the sight. Then the police tossed the only person he loved on this earth in the back of their truck like a rag doll. Just like that the video was over. The visual of his grandma being hog tied and carried out the house during a drug raid by S.W.A.T. had over three million views and counting on social media and Hope was the last to know. There was a new text message coming from his grandma's phone.

Make it easy on yourself, kid, turn yourself in. We were being nice to granny. It won't be that way for you. Then there was a smiling emoji. The message after the video was a warning. Hope looked up from his phone and knew he was all alone but not only that, the pan handler he paid to pump his gas had dashed without finishing the job.

"I'ma pop his ass," Hope said making a commitment to shoot the pan handler whenever he saw him again. Hope wiped the tears from his eyes and hopped out the car. He saw a police car ride past, but he didn't panic because the car kept going. Hope walked back to the gas tank and removed the nozzle. He watched the heavy traffic on the street in front of him.

Then Hope blanked out and his brain was promoting death. Delusional, in his mind, he saw orange flashes of gunfire in front of him, he saw the boy flash across his mind, this was the first body. The boy was crawling on the ground in the snow as bullets tore through his body, eating him alive in his quest to survive. The boy tried to crawl under a parked car to shield and prevent him from getting shot. Hope was no longer at the gas station he shot up. He stood there and he could still hear the boy's weak whimpering from underneath the parked car. God was calling him home and the boy was scared. Hope could remember the boys' legs twitching and kicking from halfway underneath the park car.

Then Hope's mind flipped the script to Christmas night when the junkie with the monkey on his back named Slim Pickins robbed him. Hope grabbed his throat because he could still feel the sharp steel slicing through his skin as Slim's cold hands ransacked his pockets. Hope still smelled his breath as he recalled the man's voice.

"That's what you want me to do huh?" Slim's voice was haunting him. Hope was reliving the event. Slim's voice continued to speak in his ear.

"Take the shit, take the shit! Huh lil' nigga why I don't hear you laughin' now? Shit ain't funny now huh?" Hope was still holding his neck filling the sharp pain. *BAH!* The gun blast and the orange lights flashed from inside Slim's mouth, making Hope flinch and he snapped back to his present, which wasn't a gift for him.

He saw people standing in the parking lot staring at him.

"What the fuck y'all looking at?" he barked at the galvanized audience. They got the message and cleared out. He stood at the gas pump on stuck mode, sweat fell down his cheek in the cold night. Hope quickly replaced the gas cap on the tank, put the nozzle back in the pump and got back in the car where shit was cool. Until Hope looked over to the right to see his dead brother, Truth, sitting in the passenger seat ready to ride.

"Let's go lil' bruh." Hope's mouth dropped at what he thought he was seeing and just heard. Hope damn near tore through the door hopping the fuck out the car.

"Ahhh!" he yelled. As people walked past, they watched and whispered about him as they went into the gas station. Hope couldn't be awake because this was the type of shit that only happened when he closed his eyes and was asleep. He looked around and stalled for a moment before he peeped back into the car.

"C'mon with this bullshit right now. I ain't got time for this shit," Hope told himself. Then he looked back in the car and Truth went back to resting in peace. While he was trying not to fall to pieces, Hope got back in the car and pulled off in search of Old School.

On a different track down in the dumps with lumps and bumps, Old School carefully walked through the town with his head hung low. His Old bones were cracking, and his body hurt as if he had been beaten with twenty baseball bats. The police had given him two black eyes, put golf ball knots all over his head and left him for dead. They put a black eye in the game for him by tarnishing his name. Old School was an authentic nigga. The man was solid as a rock, but that didn't mean nothing. His head was now on the chopping block. The weather was cold but that was nothing compared to the cold shoulder coming from the streets. His name was ringing for all the wrong reasons. See the streets are tricky, it uses tricks to get chips but under no circumstance will it accept any tricks. Old School wasn't welcome at the lion's den nor was he welcome at the snake pit or any other dope fiend hangout.

Chapter Eighteen

One day we will all be judged for what we do, for some judgement will come quicker than others. When you show up, and your every action is showcased, how will you act? Her face was unmoved in the custody of the Winnebago County Sheriff's Department.

"Come on ma'am they're waiting on you out there," the correctional officer said, as he took Hope's severely beaten grandmother's little wrinkly hand and walked the old lady from behind the gray steel bars of the dark cold concrete jail cell. The jailer helped the lady sit her sore body down in an outdated wheelchair. She was now under their jurisdiction. The overweight correctional officer wearing a tight uniform was scared to death on the inside. His sweaty pudgy hands slipped on the grips of the wheelchair Hope's grandmother's battered little body was slumped in.

"Oh, I'm sorry," he said to the notorious old lady in a nervous and apologetic tone. She looked back over her shoulder and shot him an evil eye.

"You need to be more careful," she told him weakly but in an aggressive manner. He continued pushing her in the wheelchair, his legs were shaking. His large stomach hung over his belt and started bubbling from his stressful thoughts. He had a job to do, even though the restroom was calling his name because he had to shit bad. The correctional officer had seen the old lady's face on TV ever since last night and now he had to be the person to wheel her into arraignment court.

This morning, the State of Illinois would be pointing its finger at her and formally bringing her up on indictments. They waited behind until her case was called.

"Next on the court docket. Number six, the people of the State of Illinois versus Hannah Williams," the bailiff called out.

Hope's grandma was wheeled in the courtroom handcuffed by the wrists and shackled with chains around her tiny ankles. The green and white striped jumpsuit swallowed her little body as orange flip flops on her feet set on the footrest of the outdated wheelchair. The bloody bandages on her arms and head showed she'd received some sort of medical assistance. The staples and swollen knots on her forehead were in plain view for the judge to see. Some of the people sitting in the courtroom watched her roll in with admiration in their eyes. Others despised her very existence and sat staring with a look of disgust in their faces.

Either way, they all should have paid an admission fee to see the proceedings. The courtroom was packed with news cameras from different television networks and journalists writing in their notebooks.

"Your Honor, the defendant, Hannah Williams has been charged with numerous crimes. She is facing one count of attempted murder on a peace officer in the line of duty, four counts of drug induced homicide, discharge of a firing arm with the intent to do great bodily harm, one count of unlawful use of a firing arm without a void card, one count of being a felon in possession of a firing arm, one count of resisting arrest, twenty counts of manufacturing and delivering of a controlled substance within one thousand feet of a school, church or playground. One count of being in possession of more than three thousand grams of heroin and the list of charges just keeps going on and on, with no regards to the law," read the short haired, cheap suit wearing District Attorney with her confidence going through the roof. She rolled her eyes in front of the news camera adding an over dramatic touch to her opening statements. Switching her hips, the slim, young attorney walked up to the bench with a thick folder in her hand and reached over and gave it to the judge.

Hope's grandma watched the frail DA whisper to the judge with thoughts of Old School slash Judas still on her mind. She couldn't get over believing Old School was the middleman in all this.

The packed courtroom was silent as the judge reviewed the information the D.A. had presented under oath. The glasses wearing appointed judge appeared to be a conservative republican. She was an old white lady in her mid-sixties with gray hair. She fingered the papers briefly reading the material and when she finished the judge looked up from the folder with a frown and looked down on Hope's grandma through her reading glasses.

"Uh, excuse me, Your Honor," said Hope's grandma's paid attorney as he flashed a slick smile and newly purchased white teeth.

"With all due respect for the courts, my client and I are fully aware of all the alleged charges she is facing because it's my job to know. However, Your Honor, we are here today, on this beautiful morning to set a bond for my client so can we please move right along and set a bond?" The sharp dressed attorney wore a dark Italian designer suit and made his presence known. He looked over at Hope's grandma and nodded his head as a gesture to let her know she would be out soon.

Meanwhile, an unannounced man who wore a cheaper suit walked in the courtroom and made his way over to the District Attorney's side for a short chit chat. From the looks of things, he was there on official business. The shocking look on her confident face spoken volumes.

"I'm sorry Your Honor, but may I approach the bench?" she asked the judge. This caught Hopes grandma's lawyer off guard. The judge motioned for the District Attorney to come forth. She waved goodbye to Hope's grandma as she walked by, switching her hips up to the judge and handed over another folder from the un-announced man. People in the courtroom began to whisper under their breath. Something serious was now occurring at the bench. "What's going on? I'm ready to post bail," Hope's grandma said to her lawyer. He was *shook* too. This was an irregular procedure, but the unannounced man looked real familiar to him. Though now he was wondering why the District Attorney and judge were in a long-drawn-out discussion, depriving his client of her due process.

"Say something," she ordered her attorney.

"Your Honor may I also approach the bench?" he asked with a puzzled look on his face for the news cameras. The judge acted as if she hadn't heard a word he said. So, he tried to intervene again but with much more authority in his voice.

"Your Honor! May I also approach the bench? I feel like me and my client are being left out in the cold," he said rubbing his hands over his arms as though he was shivering cold, which made the people in the audience laugh. Aside from the jokes and laugh-ter he was becoming nervous and was thinking of certain amend-ments to use as ammunition to counterpunch whatever they were about to throw at him.

"Your Honor!" the attorney beckoned again. The judge put up her hand indicating for him to 'shut the fuck up' That's when the District Attorney walked away from the bench and the judge decided to address the matter.

"Unfortunately, my hands are tied, and I must let this case go. The United States of America has a strong interest in your client sir and with that being said, bond is denied. The inmate must remain in custody while we transition her case over to the federal courts." The judge kept it short and sweet. The audience gasped in disbelief.

"Wait, wait, Your Honor. Article…" the judge slammed the wooden gavel down on his argument, meaning she didn't want to hear about an article in the newspaper, law book, or magazine.

"Your Honor…Your Honor!" he continued to yell over all the noise in the courtroom. The correctional officer went to wheel Hope's grandma back to her cold jail cell.

"It's over granny, you done had your day in court," he said with a newfound cockiness. The once scared correctional officer wasn't so scary anymore as he tugged on the wheelchair making her ride rough back to the cell. He was disrespecting her the whole way back and mumbling, "Fucking drug dealer, you're going to rot in here!" He laughed. Hope's grandma held her head low as if she'd accepted the fact that the punk ass correctional officer was right but inwardly, she had a surprise of her own for him.

"If I go, you gotta go, too," she faintly told him and began to poke him repeatedly in the stomach using an object she had hidden on her. The old woman was getting covered in blood, the carefully made shank had worked as she talked the correctional officer through his impromptu surgery.

"Keep talking shit," she told him, but he couldn't hear her because he was panicking, and his heart was pumping so fast which made the blood squirt even faster out the stab wounds. While still in handcuffs she was letting his smart ass have it as he continued to scream himself to death.

"Ahh, ahh, ahh!" the CO yelled. Police came running from everywhere in the building to his aid, but it was too late, the damage was done by the time they reached him. He was gurgling on his own blood trying his best to breathe.

"You old bitch!" one of the police yelled and they all attacked her.

"Ahh, ahh! Fuck you! Fuck you! Ahh, ahh!" she screamed as she was being punched and stomped on by several police officers.

"Ah, ahh!" The police stomped her out cold, but she was still breathing which meant she was still alive to face the new murder charge.

'I can't believe this," said one of the officers in dismay as they all stood over the dead correctional officer and the old gangster lady handcuffed and shackled lying next to him as he laid covered in blood, unconscious.

"C'mon, let's—" spoke another one of the policemen before he was interrupted by his fellow officer.'

"Don't you say it. We're not killing anybody, okay? She'll be tried in court," said another one of the officers.

"Are you serious?" the original officer asked.

Chapter Nineteen

They settled their differences overnight in the bedroom. In the streets, most relationships seemed to always work themselves out that way. The rough stuff was over, and it came to a point Wiggles and Ke-Ke were out riding around the town making it known they were fucking each other. Wiggles' cousin let them use one of his cars. It wasn't new but the Desert Sand Brown 2001 Mercedes-Benz E320 Wagon with peanut butter leather seats rolling on 23 Chrome Margo wheels and Yokohama tires to meet the streets requirements had them riding slick.

Because they'd both been struck by bullets, they shared a bottle of 750 ml Patron Silver Tequila to remedy the pain. They were riding along, switching lane to lane. Ke-Ke was in the passenger seat watching music videos on the JVL TV installed in the front console and listening to the ground pounding three fifteen-inch subwoofers. While Wiggles gripped the wooden steering wheel guiding the way, he was turning corners the right way and sliding down every hot block.

"Is that?" he questioned himself, "Hell yeah," Wiggles confirmed to himself what and who he thought he saw. So, Wiggles hit a block and pulled down on him. Wiggles pushed the button to make the window drop.

"Old School! Aye, Old School!" Wiggles yelled from the car as he turned the music down simultaneously. Old School before even looking back to see who was calling him, almost jumped out of his skin and took off running for his life.

"Tha' fuck wrong with Old School?" Wiggles said to himself, looking confused.

"Aye! Aye, Old School, it's Wiggles!" he yelled again hanging his body halfway out the car window.

"Old School!" Wiggles saw him slow down, so he drove up to meet him. "Damn, Old School, you cool?" Wiggles asked him as he noticed how hard Old School was breathing.

"You need to leave them squares alone. Your ass was going nowhere quick. Ha, ha, ha, ha," Wiggles said laughing at Old Schools slow attempt to flee and elude him.

"Fuck you, Wiggles," Old School replied as he seemingly almost coughed up both lungs.

"Old School, whatcha' doing on this side of the bridge?" Wiggles asked Old School who was still pulling himself together and pulled out a cigarette as if disregarding Wiggles' advice.

"Shit you know me," he said, coughing and getting his swag back as he lit the square. Old School blew out the smoke and relaxed his nerves. "I just left 'ah eater," he used as the reasons for his location. Wiggles laughed and looked over at Ke-Ke. She rolled her eyes and just shook her head at the comment made by Old School.

"But naw, Wiggles I need to holler at you," Old School said with his eyebrow high on his forehead making a serious face to let Wiggles know shit was real. Wiggles looked back at Ke-Ke again and then back at Old School.

"Get in," Wiggles invited him to get in the Benz wagon. Old School looked around as if he was making sure the coast was clear. He took a few more quick puffs of the generic cigarette and flicked it down hard to the street and then he looked around again with a snake look in his eyes before he opened the back door, then he got in. Once he was in the car Wiggles rolled up the window and pulled off from where he was parked.

"What's up Old School? What you got to holla at me about, huh?" Wiggles asked looking at him in the back seat through the rearview mirror.

"You know who shot 'cha?" he asked Wiggles as Ke-Ke sat up in her seat and looked back at him.

"You know who shot us, old man!" she blurted out.

Wiggles quickly pulled the car over to the side of the street, another car swerved around them angrily hitting their car horns. But before Wiggles said anything Old School had answered his own question.

"Hope." Wiggles and Ke-Ke looked at each other dumbfounded because that didn't make any sense to them at all.

"I ain't into it with that nigga," Wiggles confessed and then he sternly looked at Ke-Ke. "Bitch, you fuckin' that nigga or something?"

She made an ugly face and shook her head no.

"Hell nah, why would I be fuckin' him? Wiggles huh? I ain't just out here fuckin' everything," Ke-Ke said to her defense.

"Bitch, he ain't just shooting at us for no muthafuckin' reason!" Wiggles barked, pointing his finger in her face.

For man without a plan to save his life, this plan he conjured up from the back seat was working out perfectly for Old School. He was a straight dirt bag, his dirtbag antennas went up on the top of his head, now it was time to add more fuel to the fire he'd created.

"Nah, Wiggles don't beat ya bitch, mane," Old School said making Ke-Ke stop arguing with Wiggles, then she looked at him crazy. "No disrespect lil' mama, but this shit ain't cha' fault," he said cleaning that up real quick. "I heard you was running ya mouth on shit you had no business in, ya dig? Puttin' people and the police all in his mix. Mmm-hmm, that's what they out here sayin' my lil' nigga. When they told me, I said you wouldn't do no sucha thing, you weren't cut from that cloth but then they say he shot y'all. I was like, damn, not my main man, anybody but him. I told them if you pulled through, Hope lil' ass was in trouble 'cause my man's shoot 'dem pistols, too. You feel me?" he said patting Wiggles on the shoulder and painting the picture he wanted him to see. "But dog, I'm finna get outta here. I thought you should know. You my man and I need you out here, so do what you gotta do to live baby. I'm outta here," Old School told him, bust the back door down and got out of there. Wiggles pulled off like a bat out of hell.

"He shot at me and missed, his ass through. I'm finna kill 'dis nigga!" Wiggles said making plans in his head to leave Hope dead. "I just seen the hoe-ass nigga last night in front of cuz' house. I wish I woulda knew this shit then."

"Wiggles, he wasn't trying to kill those guys at the gas station or shoot me. Uh-huh, all those bullets had your name on them." Ke-Ke came to the new revelation. She had a good head on her shoulders, and she wanted to keep it that way. Ke-Ke wasn't a fool, it was time to jump ship. She'd seen exactly how Hope's crazy ass got down and she knew Wiggles did too. She liked Wiggles but she didn't like him enough to get killed with him. Wiggles pulled out his pistol and set it on his lap. As he drove, Ke-Ke's heart was pumping fast, she knew the frown drawn on Wiggles' face meant it was about to go down again.

"Wiggles, please drop me off before you do this," she pleaded with him in hopes he would listen to her. Wiggles looked over at her and his frown turned into a smile because she was thinking how he was thinking. He knew he didn't need any witnesses to tell on him.

"Where you trying to go?" he asked.

"To my mom's house on Sixth Street," she said giving him the *coordinates* to her safety.

"Okay cool," he said and busted a right turn getting her exactly where she needed to be. Wiggles cranked the music up and smashed the gas petal to get her out his presence fast, so he could clap Hope's ears together.

> *Heavy metal lift them up*
> *Foo 'nem gun slangin' MAC-II shaking up, like it's gan banging*
> *Bail out the steamer dump 'em down, It's lane swayin'*
> *Catch you gang banging, now yo hood famous.*
> *Off a perky walking loafing*
> *You must wanna die/ Even hoes know it ain't safe,*
> *Man, I wouldn't even lie*
> *You try to rob you six feet under*
> *We ain't eye to eye*
> *Get to that bread, watch it rise.*

Meanwhile, Old School lit another square filling a bit more at ease. "This ain't Hollywood but I'm playing on these squares," he said, blowing out the cigarette smoke at the same time. Because he'd put the bullshit in motion, now all he had to do was lay low and wait for Wiggles to score. Time was ticking, so he crept out of sight like a thief in the night.

Chapter Twenty

The streets took care of the real street niggas. There was madness all around him, so Hope was left to the streets. Hope tossed and turned on a torn couch. He'd been having his normal nightmares in the crowded smokehouse. The strong funk and crack smoke lingered in the air like a dark cloud. Paranoid crackheads stood on security for him with specific orders. Before he'd laid down to sleep, Hope had blessed the owner of the joint with the best dope. He'd given the man a half ounce of straight drop that would almost make a man's heart stop or make him come close to having a stroke. Hope knew that shit would have them peeping in and out of windows and on lock jaw stuck for hours.

All through the smokehouse the sound of crack rocks sizzling in glass pipes from being burned by high flames from rigged Bic lighters, meant the chase for a high was on. Many walks of life were all under one roof. For instance, standing isolated over in the corner of the dining room was a but naked female feeling intensively erotic but suffering from famine, she was smoking on a crack pipe religiously. While across the room from her, she was being stalked by a registered sex offender with hawk eyes and who appeared lovesick, he was yanking real hard on his dick trying to get it to spit.

In the living room the conditions were no better, garbage was everywhere. The floor looked like the ground at a landfill, hypes were rummaging through the trash, some were checking the floor for pieces of imaginary rocks they thought they might have dropped. Then sitting in the kitchen at the table were two fallen stars who drank from a forty-ounce bottle of Old English Malt Liquor. They were reminiscing about the Old Testament, talking about foxy business, and coming close to having a fallout over who had the best technique when it came to re-cooking crack in a spoon.

Down the hall, past the bathroom, somebody was sitting on the toilet taking a shit with no tissue insight. In the background, with the door halfway closed, was a lot of grunting and moaning penetrating the hallway. Three water-deprived niggas with missing teeth were in a room stretching out some white girl. And those niggas weren't playing games. They were in the room musty and sweating, they were pumping on her hard, knocking down the girl's weak vagina walls leaving a vacancy. Her eyes were wide because one of them was busting through her back door breaking the frame and ripping it off the hinges. While the other dope fiend was making her hiccup on his dick to minimize the high-pitched screaming, she continued to moan. They all were high on drugs, having a fantastic time passing 'the virus' around to each other. While in their minds living out their fantasy, when they were giving themselves a raw deal for real.

Meanwhile back up front, the afternoon news was on the TV. Hope slept on the couch and hadn't heard a thing. The breaking news involved his grandma. They had her mug shot in the background as the newscasters reported on the latest event. A Black man in a nice suit, held a microphone as he stood outside the courthouse in front of an ambulance.

"Court date turned judgment day describes the horrific turn of events here today. Our inside sources confirmed two are dead inside the courthouse. Right now, the information I've received is, at least one inmate and one correctional officer is dead. I repeat two people have died in the Winnebago County Justice Center. We will have more tonight when we receive additional details."

Chapter Twenty-one

The police sitting on guard at the hospital had become hot headed about the disturbing news from the TV. They sat in Maytag's hospital room watching the Black man in the nice suit who talked into the microphone as he stood outside the courthouse in front of an ambulance.

"Court date turned judgment day describes the horrific turn of events here today…" They all stood up and surrounded the TV hanging on the wall. Maytag still was laying in the hospital bed all fucked up over his missing legs, so he couldn't care less about them blocking his view. His life was all fucked up now and whatever happened at the courthouse didn't have anything to do with him. Matter of fact, his legs, well, what was left of his legs, were in pain. He was pressing the little call button they gave him to alert the nurses when he needed some assistance. He kept pushing the button, but nobody came to his distress call.

"Ah, aah…" Maytag groaned in pain. Not one police officer in that room looked back at him. Their eyes and ears were glued to that nigga talking on the TV.

"Our inside sources confirmed two are dead inside the courthouse. Right now, the information I've received is at least one inmate and one correctional officer is dead." Every White police officer's skin turned light red in the room. They didn't wait for the news reporter on the TV to complete what he had to say before they began making derogatory outbursts in anger over their fallen soldier's life.

Maytag's little legs were hurting him bad.

"Aah, where tha fuck the nurses at! My muthafuckin' legs are killin' me! I need some muthafuckin' medicine in this bitch!" he yelled at the top of his lungs trying to get some medical attention. But every officer turned their head in his direction and every single one of them had a deranged look on their face. Maytag suddenly shrunk in the bed and became overwhelmed with puppy eyes. His neck tingled and goosebumps popped up on the skin of his arms. The attention he needed wasn't about to be the attention he was going to get. One officer looked at the other four men in the room, then he slowly eased near the entrance door and stopped right in front of it. Maytag's thumb was pressing the button what seemed like over one hundred times for the nurses to come to the room.

"Man, c'mon…what y'all on?" he asked, still desperately pressing his thumb on the button even harder, for help.

"I ain't got no legs! I ain't got no legs! Y'all can't do this to me!" Maytag said helplessly on the verge of weeping.

The angry bloodthirsty police in Maytag's hospital room didn't give a fuck about his tears, pleas, or legs, they were surrounding him and steady putting on black leather gloves. Disabled and lying in the bed at a disadvantage, the catheter inserted into his dick couldn't control the heavy flow of piss going through the tube which caused an overflow and spilled all over the place.

"You's a nasty son of a bitch," said one of the biggest cops in the room as he and the other cops inched closer and closer to his bed.

"Y'all ain't gotta do this!" Maytag continue to sob.

"And y'all didn't have to kill a cop!" the big cop said and swung. The cop hit Maytag so hard, it sounded like a car accident was happening in the hospital room. While the other officers flinched, the passersby in the hallway paused.

"Did you just hear that?" asked one random person.

"No, come on, we're already late," the passersby cut the small talk extra short and continued to walk to their appointment.

Maytag's head instantly swole and his ears were ringing, but he was still barely conscious. It was another cop's turn, and he, same as the other cop, showed no mercy.

"Black fucker," he said gritting his teeth. He punched Maytag so many times that his co-conspirators had to pull him off his ass.

"You're going to kill him," said the big cop. Blood splattered over the white sheets in the bed. "Wake up buddy. Can you hear me?" the big cop asked. Then he swung on Maytag again making it sound like another car collision in the room.

"I said wake up," the big cop told him, but Maytag did just the opposite. He went straight to sleep, his head dropped, and blood poured from his face. The police stood around him looking at their dirty work.

"C'mon guys, let's go take a break. While we're gone anybody could've come in here, right?" the big cop said as if he'd made a true comment.

"Right."

"Right. Yeah, anybody could've come in here. Maybe somebody who wanted to fuck him up like this!"

One of the other four cops broke out in laughter first, then they all laughed amongst themselves as they headed out the door patting each other on the back.

Cap was walking with his momma when they passed by five happy police officers coming out of somebody's hospital room. He figured whoever was in that room must have done what he did and told on somebody to make them feel that way.

"Mama," he said as he continued to walk down the hall with his arm hanging in a sling.

"What Cap?" said Cap's mom.

"Can you go get the car? I want to see my girl before I leave." She looked at him and shook her head.

"Yeah, okay boy, but hurry up. I gotta go to the club tonight. Messin' 'round with you, you been makin' me miss money," she told him and walked off to get the car from the parking lot. Cap walked the halls until he reached his girlfriend's door.

"This shit's crazy," he said and opened the door. When Cap walked in, he was caught by surprise to see her eyes open.

"Baby you woke?" he asked as he walked to her bedside.

"Cap, did you get him? Did you get that money, huh?" she asked him in her strained voice as she peered at him through her swollen black eyes. Cap could see she had so much faith in him, so deep down on the inside he didn't want to tell her the truth. He'd dropped the ball and Hope's name to the cops. He stood there with his head held down. She reached out and laid her hand on his head to comfort him. That's when he broke down and started crying which made her shed tears.

"Cap baby, it's okay, it's okay, fuck that nigga. You had to kill 'em, look what he did to me."

Cap paused in the middle of a sniffle. She had just sniped his gangster. He lifted his head and looked deeply into her eyes. She stared and could see something was wrong with Cap. He took her hand from his head and held it in his. She continued to look in his eyes.

"What, Cap?" He squeezed her hand.

"I love you," he told her.

"I love you, too, Cap." Then he had to do something he wasn't used to.

"Umm…I couldn't get 'em. The police got to me first." She looked at him confused.

"Cap, whatcha talkin' about?"

"They made me tell on him, he did you so bad. They wanted to know who he was."

"And you told 'em!" she snapped. It was over. She snatched her hand away from him and even though the pain was horrific she turned her swollen head toward the other wall so she didn't have to look at him and cried.

"Get out! You bitch ass nigga!"

There was nothing else he could do but respect her wishes. Cap walked out the door disgraced.

Chapter Twenty Two

Oftentimes, the niggas in the streets participated in bringing forth their own demise while choosing to pass the blame to someone else. In the current scenario, Hope was the fall guy. Wiggles failed to acknowledge his involvement due to his own self-inflicted anger and pain. Truth be told, he was part to blame for the bullet holes he'd received in his body. In his mind, it was either going to be Hope's or his eulogy that was going to be heard in front of everybody in a church.

And as for Wiggles, being persuaded by Judas, AKA Old School, it was time for him to go back to simple street fundamentals and put in some work. Wiggles had decided somebody was going to die behind him getting shot. Wiggles thought to himself, *in Hope's family, it was going to be a two for one today.* Like Hope's grandma, many hours passed away and they were never coming back. A deadly day was going to turn into a nonexistent night.

Wiggles was upset after he'd realize he was wearing Hope's patchwork. He moved in the cold night dressed in all-black ready to attack on hunt mode with death in his eyes. Wiggles was rolling in a low-key car behind tinted windows carrying a Tec 9-millimeter and .10 millimeter pistol for the ride along. He was driving past every gas station, every liquor store, looking for Hope. Wiggles knew if Hope found him again it would be another incident and he couldn't afford to keep taking bullets at the cost of losing his own life. So, with that in mind, there was no need to hesitate. He wasn't about to become a long-term resident at the cemetery.

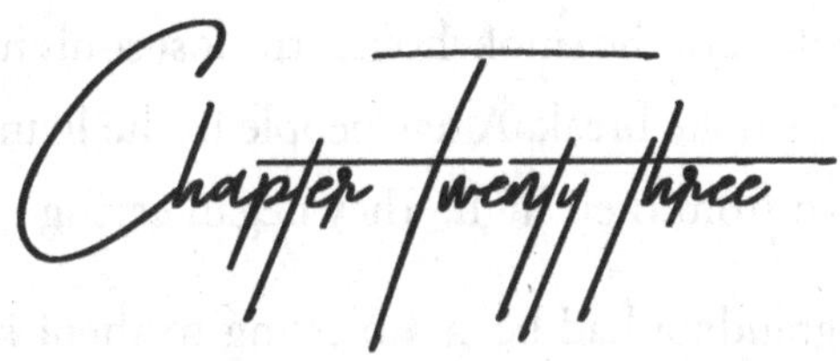

Chapter Twenty Three

"Yeah, my man they killed her in jail. She dead. The shit been on TV all day, ain't none of y'all niggas seen shit?"

"Nah," said one of the junkies in the room.

"Man, how long Hope been in there sleep?"

"All day," another junkie replied.

"Tha fuck y'all saying? He don't know?"

"We didn't know, how the fuck he gonna know?"

The bearer of bad news's face looked spooked.

"Nigga, gimme my dope back. You think I'm finna stick around here when dat boy wake up! Um, shit." He got out that jam just on principle.

The talk around town was Hope was beating people with pistols just for looking at him wrong and now there were also whispering about him killing a boy. As the deadly news traveled through the door of the smokehouse, the lost souls fucking around had to take a smoke break. A few people in the living room began to breakdown from their high. They began crying.

Hope's grandma had been a blessing to them in their cursed lives. She was the only person they could go to for help. Those days were now over. Hope woke up in a moment of silence, feeling uneasy. The sound of weeping overcame the house, and he knew there was no more sleeping for him. Hope sat up and started wiping his eyes and stretching out his arms. He paused with his arms out as he noticed every teary eye in the house was focused on him.

"What happened?" The lost souls stood around hesitating to come forth. Hope stood up checking his pockets making sure his money, dope, and pistol were still in his possession. He noticed a naked chick looking at him crazy as she was putting on her clothes in a hurry. Then he heard a knock at the door, but nobody moved.

"Hope sit back down. I gotta tell you something, and I don't know how," said the bearer of bad news. The serious conversation was interrupted by yelling and heavy pounding coming from an intoxicated man on the other side of the door.

"Let me in this muthafucka!" said the yelling man. The voice sounded familiar to everybody in the smokehouse including

Hope. His eyes got wide with surprise and his heart was pounding hard and fast with excitement.

"I said goddamnit, let me in this muthafucka. I ain't told on that old bitch, I ain't told on that old bitch y'all. Y'all hear me, I ain't never told on a muthafuckin' soul, goddamnit I'm Old School!"

Hope was pulling the .44 revolver from his hip when the TV sitting in front of him flashed his grandma's mug shot with the word deceased under it.

"Huh?" was all Hope managed to say and that word left his mouth taking his breath away.

Somebody, who seemed very smart, opened the door to run so they could save their own life. At the same time, Old School's drunk ass was barging in to lose his. Hope's eyes crossed when he saw Old School. He didn't even see it coming.

"That old bitch done lied—"

Hope pulled the trigger. BAH! BAH! The 44-revolver barked loudly, but the bites were worse. People held their hands over their ears and flinched with each gun blast. Old School instantly dropped on the living room floor in front of the TV. He was gazing up at the mugshot grunting. Hope wasn't trying to hear a word he had to say. Tears fell from Hope's eyes as he looked at his grandma's picture.

"They killed my grandma nigga, because of you!" Blood was spurting from the two shots in Old School's stomach.

Old School was still trying to speak but couldn't get a word out due to coughing. Hope kicked him across the mouth, and then finished Old School off pointing the gun directly in his face, pulling the trigger again.

BAH! BAH! BAH! Flesh, brains, cartilage, and skull fragments from Old School's head exploded all over the trashy floor. Blood splatter was all over Hope's clothes, and the TV. During the shooting, people were screaming and running out the house. Hope looked around the empty smokehouse and slowly backed-pedaled out the opened door, looking confused.

The cold night air woke him up as it hit his face. Hope stood outside holding the .44 revolver. He pulled the bloody white hoodie over his head to hide his face. He tucked the gun and ran to the car parked behind the smokehouse. His breathing was so heavy that cold air could be seen leaving his nostrils and mouth under the streetlight in the alley. Hope's adrenaline was at an all-time high and his tears were overflowing.

"Grandma, what I'ma do?" he cried, standing at the car fumbling through his pockets for the keys. In the distance, junkies and crackheads silhouettes were seen running in the dark. Hope heard them saying his name over the sounds of the police sirens in the background. Hope found the keys and unlocked the car door.

"C'mon, c'mon," he said, motivating himself to get out of there. The honest to gods' truth was he was scared as fuck. He had nobody else in his family alive.

He was the last of a dying breed. The car cranked on, and Hope closed the door. He took the .44 revolver off his hip and threw it in the passenger seat. A few blocks ahead, he saw red and blue flashing lights. The heavy bass shook the trunk from the music and was pounding the ground and rocking the block.

It wuz a murda, 'cuz I'm like the reaper

And make a nigga,

See the flatline aggravated murda, destroyin' all competition

and niggaz

Thinkin', they can take mine, it wuz a murda, Cuz I murda my foes

And left a nigga full of bullet holes cuz they thought it was sweet, I pack heat,

puttin niggaz to sleep/ my eyes red, from the weed I chief

Hope didn't turn the music down because there was no time for that. He was trying to get out that jam, so he busted a move. He put the car in reverse and was backing out the parking space while at the same time reaching his hand under the driver's seat for his other heat just in case he had to put somebody else to sleep when he peeped a limping nigga coming towards his car, but before he could recognize the person, shots were fired at him.

Lurking in the dark in search of Hope, Wiggles found exactly who he had been looking for all night. PAP! PAP! PAP! PAP! PAP! Wiggles was pulling on the trigger of the tech 9-millimeter letting Hope have it. PAP! PAP! PAP! PAP! PAP! Bullets were flying violently through windows and car doors. PAP! PAP! PAP! PAP! PAP! Hope was quick to duck low and smash his foot on the gas pedal.

"Ahh! Ahh! Muthafucka!" he yelled, in the car. The cutlass darted backwards making Wiggles dive out the way. Hope hurried up and slammed the gear shift and drive, then before he knew it, more gunshots were exploding in the alley.

"Ahh!" Hope hollered, because this time he was struck in the back of his shoulders by a bullet. Out of desperation, Hope took the gun he was reaching for and started letting it ride through the driver's door window.

POP! POP! POP! POP! POP! Glass shattered all over him cutting his face. He hit the gas and the car took off straight. Wiggles jumped up and was running with the car gunning it down. PAP! PAP! PAP! He wasn't about to let Hope get out of there alive.

PAP-PAP! The shot-up Cutlass was snatching down the alley and still getting hit up.

"Bitch," Hope said gritting his teeth as he stuck the gun out the window and returned fire. POP-POP-POP-POP! The Glock .40 was jumping in his hand from the recoil. Hope didn't know who the nigga was shooting at him, but he saw dude drop by some garbage cans from one of the shots, knocking them over. When Hope saw that, instantaneously, he stomped his feet on the brakes. He wasn't about to take a chance. Whoever this was, he was about to dance with the devil tonight and leave the earth with him.

"Muthafuck," Hope said, looking at the blood-stained white hoodie from where he had been shot. Hope stayed low for cautious reasons. He was trying to hear if any more gunshots were going to be sent his way before he opened the car door.

"Who da fuck is this?" Hope said, mad as fuck as he got out the car not quite yet feeling the burning sensation from the hot lead lodged in his shoulder. The rest of the glass from the shot-out window fell out his lap. In the distance, the sound of the police sirens were getting closer and closer so Hope knew he had to make it quick. He ran down the alley towards the fallen garbage cans and the closer he got, the madder he became because clearly, he could see the shooter was Wiggles.

"Nigga, you wanna play crazy?" Hope said and shot him. POP!

"Aah!" Wiggles screamed in pain lying stretched out over some busted black garbage bags.

"Nigga you's a bitch!" POP! Hope told him and shot him again. Although Wiggles was trapped under the gun, he was still trying to grab the Tech .9 millimeter he'd dropped from getting hit in the same shoulder as before. Hope was looking at him in amazement.

"Get the fuck outta here. Whatcha' tryin' to do?" Hope asked him and laughed at the same time. Hope found a lot of humor in Wiggles' actions.

"Stupid muthafucka," Hope mumbled to himself and kicked the gun far out of Wiggles' reach.

"Fuck you, fuck you, fuck you, Hope!" Wiggles yelled at Hope as he laid in between the disgusting and foul-smelling garbage cans. Hope walked over and kneeled near him to get up close and personal with Wiggles. Hope could see the man's breath floating in the night from panic and fright. Hope looked Wiggles in his eyes while talking to him.

"Do you know me? Huh? Nah, you don't, but you got my muthafuckin' name in yo' mouth," Hope told him and snatched the gold chain Wiggles was wearing from around his neck. "I don't wanna get no blood on this."

"My cousin gonna get you for this," Wiggles warned him. Hope stood up, leaned over and shoved the pistol into Wiggles' cheek.

"Aah!" he screamed. Hope looked at Wiggles squirming with a gun to his face then enlightened him on what this shit was all about.

"You know what Wiggles? It's ya mouth," Hope said.

"Fuck you, nigga!" Wiggles yelled. Hope pushed the gun harder into his cheek.

"It's ya mouth and fuck yo' cousin," Hope repeated himself and thought about the loss of his grandma. POP! He shot Wiggles in the face and paused. Wiggles' eyes rolled to the top of his head, indicating he was dead.

"I just lost my grandma. Bitch!" Hope kept the gun pointed at Wiggles' leaking head and let his index finger squeeze on the trigger repeatedly. POP! POP! POP! POP! POP! Hope finished nailing Wiggles right there in the garbage and ran back to the high-performance Cutlass. The music was still slamming hard in the trunk and gray smoke was coming from the rumbling Magnaflow dual exhaust, ready to run. Hope hopped in, slammed the door, and smashed his foot hard on the gas. The letter tires spun so fast getting out of there. The car jumped over bumps and potholes as it scooted through the alley. His mind was gone with the loud music blasting in his ear along with hallucinations of deceased Slim's voice silently haunting and taunting him.

"You know what, you're a lucky muthafucka. I ain't gonna kill ya lil' ass, only because it's Christmas. I'ma let you live. But I better not catch ya ass on this block no more. Now nod your head if you understand what tha fuck I just said, shorty." Hope was nodding his head to the dead man's command living in the past but going super-fast in real life, fishtailing out the alley into the main street where the police were parked fifteen deep in front of the smokehouse. The bullet hole decorated Cutlass with the fifteen-inch subwoofer's banging in the trunk zoomed past the flashing red and blue lights, lightning up the night in the opposite direction going about seventy miles per hour, grabbed their attention. The police Sergeant put two and two together and sent four plus three police squad cars on Hope's ass.

"Follow that car! That might be our shooting suspect!" he yelled through the radio waves and just like that, a high-speed chase ensued with Hope being the underdog. Eager for a kill and the thrill for a notch on the gun handle of their service pistols, made the police officers show no restraint, it was time to go hard in the paint. This was the stuff legends were made from. This was the type of shit they lived for. This is where all the repetitious training came into play. The seven police cars quickly got into formation and began their pursuit through the relentless Rockford streets.

Hope was heavily sweating and feeling lightheaded. He was losing blood, punching the gas, and whipping the front end of the vehicle for real. The car took off like a rocket, as if it was one, the Magnaflow dual exhaust howling like a wolf seeing the moon. The car was moving but he still could see in the rearview mirrors the red and blue flashing lights trailing him.

"Yeah, I see you. Bye-bye I'm outta here," Hope said then he went to performing. The high-performance Cutlass' speed went from zoom to vroom. Hope turned corners damn near on two wheels, *skit skirt!* The squealing tires, along with the loud police sirens, woke people up who were laying in their beds in their homes. Then something in Hope's disturbed head clicked which sent him off his rockers. Hope's face frowned up. He started talking aloud to himself.

"Y'all killed my grandma, huh?" he spoke the truth and then felt the urgency to shoot. Hope used one hand to guide the steering wheel and the other hand to change the clip in the Glock .40 to replace the extended magazine with a full extended clip.

"Yeah, yeah, yeah," he was using self-talk as encouragement, to boost his own adrenaline, while smiling like a gremlin. Hope eased his foot off the gas pedal which caused the Cutlass to lose speed while he raised the gun across his bloody body and let it rest in the broken window on top of the door panel. The chill of the ice-cold wind whipped through the cuts in his face but it was making him feel alive. One of the anxious and thirsty brave cops who lead the team on the car chase, quickly saw an opportunity to show off. Unknowing, the brave cop was about to get his head blown the fuck off as he slid on the side of Hope's car. The hero cop was driving on the side of Hope as he waved his arm and motioned for him to pull the car over and stop. But in his heroic act he had been totally oblivious to the large barrel of the .40 caliber resting on the car door and pointing straight at him.

"Pull over! Pull over! Pull over, goddamnit!" the cop was yelling. The cop's needs to play dirty grew so he went in getting ready to ram Hope and the car off the road. Soon as the police car was about to make contact with the Cutlass, Hope waited until it was close enough and went to busting the gun. POP! POP! POP!

POP! POP! POP! POP! The hot shit Hope sent over there went through the squad car and knocked the man's top off making his brain splash on the windshield as he lost his grip on life and the steering wheel.

The view from behind made a following female officer in the chase want to reconsider her occupation and choose a new career.

"Oh, shit! Are you freaking kidding me?" she shouted in her car as she watched the action ahead of her. The other police in their squad cars who trailed behind Hope couldn't believe what they saw.

"Oh my God! Shots fired! Shots fired! Officer down!" she frantically screamed over the radio back to base for the whole calvary to join in on the high-speed chase. She and the other police officers saw orange gunfire exit the window of Hope's bullet riddled Cutlass. The gunfire was introduced to the speeding lead squad car and into three parked civilian cars, which caused a loud collision.

Hope watched the car accident from his rearview mirror. Then he hit the gas and the car went back racing down the street.

"Who next? Ha, ha, ha!" he asked while laughing at their scary asses. "Huh, who next muthafuckas?" Hope was yelling in excitement. The seven original police cars chasing him were reduced to six and he still had more shots in the new clip, and he had more clips where that came from. Hope began to check their temperature and like before he eased his foot off the gas pedal.

"C'mon, c'mon, I got something for you," he was taunting them, but they slowed down too, fronting their move. "Huh, y'all sum' bitches," he said and pointed the gun out the window aiming backwards and started shooting again. POP! POP! POP! POP! POP! POP! "Who next?" he kept yelling and shooting the Glock .40. POP! POP! POP! POP! But this time was much different.

BOOM! BOOM! BOOM! Some more police had showed up and they were with the bullshit. BOOM! BOOM!

Hope ducked and he could feel the car swaying from being hit by the gunfire the police had returned. He started laughing at them and lifted his head up just a little bit to look out the back window. Then he saw a cop with S.W.A.T. written across his bullet proof vest, the cop was hanging out the window, sitting on the car door holding a .12-gauge shotgun waving his hand at Hope saying *hello*.

Hope snapped out. "Bitch!" And went back to shooting. POP! POP! POP! POP!

BOOM! BOOM! A real gun fight escalated. BOOM! BOOM! Hope stomped on the gas pedal, pushing it to the floor.

"Fuck it!" The car was already going fast at one hundred-thirty miles per hour but it jerked and the speedometer was moving pass three-digit numbers quickly. One hundred forty miles per hour, one hundred fifty-five miles per hour. BOOM! The shots kept coming. The Cutlass was running at an outstanding speed and

Hope was losing them. He was now moving at a reckless speed of one hundred sixty miles per hour.

"Y'all can't fuck with me!"

The world flew past fast and when he looked into the rearview mirror to see the distance between him and the cops, he failed to see the two cops in front of him and the two police officers working together to lay down spike strips. Hope's hallucinations returned at the wrong time to haunt him again. His eyes were still focused on the rearview mirror so instead of him seeing the police eating his dust for a late-night snack, the face of the first person Hope ever killed appeared in the mirror.

"Aah, what tha fuck!" Then suddenly, Hope heard a loud explosion coming from underneath his car then he lost control. The spike strips had done their job and blown out the letter tires. The aftermath sent the high-performance Cutlass flying directly into an oak tree, head on, ejecting Hope's body through the front window shield riddled with bullet holes. All the officers watched in amazement as his body went soaring into the air.

Acknowledgements

First, I want to thank God, for always being there when I thought there was no hope. There would not have been these stories had He not chosen me to go through my journey.

I acknowledge my publisher, Eartha Gatlin and my editor Megan Joseph for your drive, expertise, and ambition to collaborate with me to bring another one of my project's to life. You two are a real-life dynamic duo!

I am forever grateful to my Mom, Leona Streeter, without you, none of this would have ever been possible, and I am eternally grateful for you, my number one fan and She-ro, always and forever. And to my brother "Bug" for working on yourself, watching you lets me know we're going to be good. I acknowledge my sons, Lil Tiger and Kortae, you are the inspiration that keeps me pushing forward, I can't wait to see what's next for us.

about the author

Tyress Cunningham is the author of Conflict of Intere$t. He is a business owner. Tyress was once was a part of the problem and now he is working on being a part of the solution. He has been in jails, in prisons, and in mental institutions. For years he hung around hustlers, pimps, and prostitution. He lived in the streets and in his words, "on the streets asking for change, to now making a change! Hope you never felt like me when I was down bad. Hope you never do what I did. Hope you know that only you can save you when there's no hope."

9 780578 968018